I0782040

Nicol Williamson's Magic Skullcap

& other essays

Roger Zotti

Nicol Williamson's Magic Skullcap & other essays
Copyright © 2024 Roger Zotti

Produced and printed by Stillwater River Publications.
All rights reserved. Written and produced in the United States of America.
This book may not be reproduced or sold in any form without the expressed,
written permission of the author(s) and publisher.

Visit our website at **www.StillwaterPress.com** for more information.

First Stillwater River Publications Edition

ISBN: 978-1-963296-59-4 (paperback) / 978-1-963296-62-4 (hardcover)

Names: Zotti, Roger, author.
Title: Nicol Williamson's magic skullcap, & other essays / Roger Zotti.
Description: First Stillwater River Publications edition. | West Warwick, RI,
    USA : Stillwater River Publications, [2024]
Identifiers: ISBN: 978-1-963296-59-4 (paperback) | 978-1-963296-62-4
    (hardcover)
Subjects: LCSH: Zotti, Roger. | Celebrities. | Motion pictures. | Actors. |
    Athletes. | Boxers (Sports) | LCGFT: Essays.
Classification: LCC: PS3626.O78 N53 2024 | DDC: 814/.6—dc23

1 2 3 4 5 6 7 8 9 10

Written by Roger Zotti.
Cover and interior design by Elisha Gillette.
Published by Stillwater River Publications, West Warwick, RI, USA.

*The views and opinions expressed in this book are solely those of the author(s)
and do not necessarily reflect the views and opinions of the publisher.*

To Maryann, Tom, Leslie, Katja, Roy, and Jake

TABLE OF CONTENTS

I cannot remember when I was not reading. To stop reading would be a sort of partial death—the death of all of me which extends beyond what I can hear, taste, or touch, pretty much the whole life of the mind.
> —Dean Acheson, quoted in *Grapes from Thornes*

How does the creative impulse in us die? The English teacher who wrote fiercely on the margin of your rheme in blue pencil: 'Trite, rewrite,' helped to kill it. Critics kill it…Families are great murderers of the creative impulse, particularly husbands. Older brothers sneer at younger brothers and kill it.
> —Brenda Ueland, quoted in *If You Want to Write*

I daydream a lot when I read. For me, that's part of the pleasure of reading. A good book will trigger a memory.
> —Justin Torres, quoted in the Boston Globe

INTRODUCTION

If you want to learn about the great British actor Nicol Williamson's acting and personal life, I suggest reading Martin Dowsing's *Beware of the Actor! The Rise and Fall of Nicol Williamson* and Gabriel Hershman's *Black Sheep: The Authorised Biography of Nicol Williamson.*

Why? The essays in this book about this amazing actor (1938-2011) focus on several of his movies but not much about his personal life.

For some people, he was a handful to work with. Unreliable. Disruptive. Unpredictable. For other individuals, as you'll learn, he was decent and caring.

The other essays in this book are informative, entertaining, and readable, and, yes, if I'm writing about a book or movie, I think of the piece as a visceral reaction to what I've read or seen, not a review of it.

The boxing pieces in this book were originally published in *The International Boxing Research Organization Journal.*

Finally, you have my word you won't be tested on any of the essays in this book. My word! Honest!

SOME KINDNESS

In Joseph Thomas Moore's biography, *Larry Doby: The Struggle of American League's First Black Player,* consider how Doby's teammate Joe Gordon treated him.

The team was Bill Veeck's Cleveland Indians, the date July 5, 1947. Larry Doby was seated at the end of the dugout bench. The White Sox were leading the Indians 5-1 in the seventh inning.

Moore quotes Veeck, who pointed out that the game was Doby's first as an American Leaguer, and when he came to bat, "he swung at three pitches and missed each of them by at least a foot. He walked back to the dugout with his head down." Walking past everyone, "he sat in the corner, all alone, with his head in his hands."

That's when second baseman Joe Gordon swung into action. Here's Veeck again: "[Gordon] was the next batter and missed each of the next three pitches by at least two feet, and came back to the bench and sat down next to Doby, and put his head in his hands too....After that, every time that Doby went onto the field, he would pick up Gordon's glove and throw it to him. It's as nice a thing as I ever saw or heard of in sports."

Doby, who led the America League in homeruns in 1952 and 1954, retired from professional baseball in 1959. He was inducted into Baseball's Hall of Fame in 1998.

In 1979, he became the second black American League manager, taking over the Chicago White Sox.

On the one hundredth anniversary of his birthday, he was posthumously awarded the Congressional Gold Medal. Doby died in 2003 at age seventy-nine.

Joe Gordon, who began his baseball career with the New York Yankees in 1938, was the American League Most Valuable Player in 1942 and retired with Cleveland in 1950. He was posthumously elected to Baseball's Hall of Fame in 2009.

Turning to the world of acting, consider the late British actor Nicol Williamson. He could be rude, pugnacious, and occasionally mean, especially to other actors.

What would set him off? Maybe it was the way another actor looked, spoke, or moved. Maybe it was an actor's lack of preparation for a role.

Maybe Williamson enjoyed being a ballbreaker.

But he had moments of kindness too. For example: there's what he did concerning a friend, television producer Leslie Megahey.

In *Beware the Actor! The Rise and Fall of Nicol Williamson*, Martin Dowsing writes about the time Megahey asked Williamson for a favor. He told the actor he'd be gone for several weeks and that "you can have the entire house if you want, and all you have to do is look after [Danny] the dog," who loved Williamson.

Surprisingly, Williamson declined and said he'd stay at a hotel.

Megahey says that "when the dog died sometime later," Williamson "rang me quite late one night from Amsterdam and sang the whole of 'Danny Boy,' then quietly put the phone down."

LIGHTS OFF AND ON FOR YOGI

FIRED

A few days after the 1964 season ended, Yogi Berra met with the New York Yankees' co-owners Dan Topping and Del Webb in their office. With them was Ralph Houk, the team's former manager and current general manager.

Despite managing the Yankees to the American League pennant in his rookie season, and, as Jon Pessah writes in *Yogi: A Life Behind the Mask*, "almost a world series with an aging and injured team," Berra was fired.

And why was he fired? According to Pessah, during the season several players, without Berra's knowledge, complained to Houk that he lacked leadership, that he "can't communicate," that "he can't control the players who break the rules," and that he's "leaving the starting pitchers in too long."

None of the Yankees, Pessah continues, "ever takes a complaint to Berra. They all gripe to Houk, to one another, even to the beat writers—but never on the record [and] no one will ever take responsibility or identify which of his teammates undercut Yogi."

Regarding Houk, nicknamed "the Major" because of his rank in the marines, Pessah writes that "[he] never tells his players to take their gripes to the manager. Or to stop bitching and start playing better. Nor does he sit down with his rookie manager and tell him about the problems brewing in his clubhouse, as Topping and Webb clearly expected."

NAME THAT TUNE

DURING HIS YEARS AS A PLAYER, YOGI WAS PART OF, PESSAH writes, "a clubhouse that policed itself, a place where [veteran players] kept younger players in line....A player going to management? Behind the manager's back? Unthinkable."

Friends with his teammates, especially Mickey Mantle and Whitey Ford, Berra now had a different role.

Now he was no longer a teammate.

Now was the team's manager and boss.

Mantle and Ford were two of the major league's best players and, in 1974, entered baseball's Hall of Fame, but while they played for the Yankees, they "treated policies and curfews as suggestions rather than hard-and-fast rules."

An incident on the team bus to Boston is worth mentioning involving Phil Linz—who was playing a harmonica he had recently purchased—Mantle, Ford, Joe Pepitone, and several other players. They had broken two of Berra's rules by drinking before they boarded the bus and also while they were on it.

Berra asked Linz to stop playing the harmonica, but he didn't. The usually slow-to-anger Berra became enraged at Linz's disrespect. Approaching the player, he roared at him to "shove the harmonica up your ass" and to "play it in your damn room."

There was silence on the bus.

"Every player watches a Berra they barely recognize," Pessah writes, "including Mantle, who realizes a line has been crossed.... They have just seen Berra's tough side. He's lost his temper and—in the arrested-adolescent world of professional sports—regained much of his authority. In Mantle's mind, it was the first time he showed leadership, and he felt the difference....It was time, Mantle decides, to stop joking and make sure his teammates played hard in each of the forty-three games the Yankees have left."

...the arrested-adolescent world of professional sports...

ALL THOSE ACCOMPLISHMENTS

AMONG BERRA'S MANY ACCOMPLISHMENTS DURING HIS eighteen years with the Yankees was winning the AL's Most Valuable Player in 1951, 1954, and 1955. He played for ten New York world championship teams and in fifteen straight All-Star games, had a lifetime batting average of .285, and slammed 358 homeruns.

There's more. First, as Lorne Manley writes in a *New York Times* piece titled "Going to Bat for a Rare Gem in the Majors," in 1950, "Berra went to the plate 650 times and struck out 12 times...."

Second, "only two major leaguers have ever hit more than 350 homeruns while striking out fewer than 450 times: Joe DiMaggio and Yogi."

Third, in 1972, Berra was inducted into Baseball's Hall of Fame.

OUT AND ON

YES, THE LIGHTS WENT OUT FOR YOGI BERRA WHEN HE WAS fired as manager of the Yankees in 1964, but the next year the Yankees finished sixth, and in 1966, Pessah writes, "dead last... [and] Houk had to step in for [manager] Johnny Keane after only twenty games. The Yankees have finished higher than fourth only once since Yogi's exit, even after the league expanded in 1969 and split into two divisions composed of six teams each."

Though the franchise had fallen on hard times since his firing,

Berra never gloated, but, Pessah writes, he had to feel "vindicated"—and rightly so.

Whoa! In 1972, the lights came back on for Berra, and he became manager of the National League New York Mets. In 1973, the team won the National League pennant. He managed the Mets until 1975. In 1984 and 1985, he returned to manage the Yankees.

TEACHER, TEACHER

ALMA MATER

Nineteen fifty-six was my senior year at New Haven's Hillhouse High School, and my English teacher was called Mr. Lurk, who believed that any book written after 1925 was trash. (He pronounced the word TRASH in capital letters.)

One December morning before class, I took a deep breath, mustered whatever courage I had, approached his desk, and said, "Mr. Lurk, why don't we, er, compromise?"

He looked at me, and I realized his left eye was slightly smaller than his right one.

"What I mean is, we can read one book written before 1925, then a book written after 1925, and so on."

(I was tempted to suggest that on a regular basis we read whatever book we wanted, then write a two page paper on it, with the first paragraph being a brief synopsis and the rest of the paper devoted to two aspects of the book we thought were the most important and why—always why—but I kept my mouth shut.)

He told me he didn't compromise when it came to literature, which didn't surprise me, and that I was bordering on rudeness, and, wanting me out of his sight, he wrote something on a piece of paper and told me to bring it to the assistant principal's office.

(I sensed a touch of snarl in his voice. Be careful of people with one eye smaller than the other and a snarl in their voices.)

After the assistant principal read what he had written, he grinned and said, "Okay, now, just wait here until the bell rings and then go to your next class."

Good guy, that assistant principal.

Well, I retaliated by going on strike in Mr. Lurk's class. I only did the in-class assignments…and for some reason, he passed me for the next three marking periods with Ds. He rarely called on me in class, and when he did, I'd invent some brief bullshit response, and he'd smirk.

But the Ds didn't discourage me from reading on my own at home the likes of sports journalists Dan Parker, W. C. Heinz, Red Smith, and Budd Schulberg. In later years, I discovered Katherine Dunn's *One Ring Circus* and *Geek Love* and then Joyce Carol Oates' *On Boxing*.

FOXWOODS

ONE OF SCHULBERG'S BEST BOOKS, *THE HARDER THEY FALL*, was made into a 1954 movie starring Humphrey Bogart. (It was Bogie's last movie, and, if I correctly recall, the great Jan Sterling played Beth, his wife.)

Also, Schulberg wrote both the novel *On the Waterfront* and the screenplay for the wonderful 1954 Oscar winning movie.

A few years ago, Schulberg appeared at Foxwoods Casino to sign autographs for *Sparring with Hemingway*, his last book. He was in his early nineties, and I was amazed how good he looked.

I asked him why so many fighters didn't know when to quit fighting—champions like Ray Robinson, Joe Louis, and Willie Pep—and he said something like *they always think they have a few more good bouts in them.* An ego thing too. Maybe money problems. It comes with the territory.

I thanked him for writing *On the Waterfront*, and he signed my copy of the screenplay, and we shook hands, and I thanked him again, and off I went.

NIGHT

I THINK THE ONLY NON-SPORTSWRITER I READ THAT SENIOR Hillhouse year was Davis Grubb, the author of *The Night of the Hunter*, which was made into a memorably frightening movie about love and hate, good and evil, and greed. Its central character was a murderous preacher named Harry Powell, who Robert Mitchum played to perfection.

(This was one of Mitchum's best performances in a long career of excellent performances, and he deserved, at the least, an Oscar nomination for his turn as Powell.)

I saw the movie first, which Charles Laughton directed, then read the novel.

And, yes, I was tempted to write a short paper on the book and hand it in to Mr. Lurk and hope for extra credit, but I didn't because I knew he'd glance at my work and rip it up, because, after all, the novel was written in 1953, which axiomatically meant for him—and others of his ilk— that it was T-R-A-S-H.

WHAT STANDS OUT FOR ME (1)

About RKO's *His Kind of Woman* (1951) is Vincent Price's scene stealing performance as a hammy Hollywood actor named Mark Cardigan.

The movie also stars Robert Mitchum as Don Milner and Jane Russell as Lenore Brent, who eventually becomes Milner's love interest. In a small role, the great Charles McGraw plays a growling, well-dressed thug named Thompson and menacingly struts around ready to shoot anyone who looks too long at him.

Mitchum's Milner is a small-time gambler paid big money to go to Mexico by syndicate boss Nick Ferraro (Raymond Burr, later to achieve fame as TV's Perry Mason). In Mexico, Ferraro, the double-crossing, conniving bastard that he is, plans to murder Milner and assume his identity.

The movie is a mix of genres, beginning as a film noir, turning into a romance, and ending as an action thriller. Confusing? Yes—and that's why the critics lambasted it.

(It was one of those movies that took on a life of its own and the hell with its storyline.)

Near the end of the movie, Cardigan has a chance to save Milner's life. Aware that he's living a life of make-believe as an actor, rescuing Milner from Ferraro's thugs is his chance to prove to himself, to his fans, and to the movie-going public that he's both a hero in real life and on the big screen.

Before Cardigan, who has recruited a motley group of geezers to help him rescue Milner, reaches the gangster's yacht, a shirtless Milner tries to fight off Ferraro's thugs. Though he's tough, he's eventually subdued and even kneed in the balls—ouch!—by Ferraro, which causes our hero much distress.

(As Cardigan sets out with his geezer brigade, he utters his best line: "Praise me later!")

And you guessed it, big boss Ferraro gets what he deserves at the end of the movie.

Clearly, Price has a great time playing Cardigan, and one reason being he's given a chance to quote Shakespeare. Before he sets out to rescue Milner, he delivers a timely quote from *Hamlet*: "Now could I drink hot blood,/ And do such bitter business as the day/ Would quake to look upon."

Price admitted he loved every hammy second of playing a hammy actor.

. . . in Larry Carli's *The Top Ten Middleweight Champions* (2017) is the section titled "Ring Greats Who Never Got A Shot at the Title." Carli cites Harry "Kid" Matthews.

What a talented light heavyweight Matthews was!

A bout between him and the great Archie Moore would've been a boxing fan's dream fight come true.

Instead of pressing to arrange a light heavyweight title fight with champion Joey Maxim, Jack Hurley, Matthews' manager, matched him against Rocky Marciano, the winner to fight heavyweight champion Jersey Joe Walcott.

Mistake.

Yankee Stadium. July 27, 1952. Though Matthews won the opening round, one of most powerful and accurate left hooks

Marciano ever landed caught the Seattle, Washington, fighter in round two and flattened him.

A superb boxer-puncher—and a pleasure to watch in action—Matthews was never quite the same after his loss to Marciano.

He fought from 1937 to 1956 and retired with a record of 90-7-6 (61 KOs/ 3 KO 'by).

…in Joey Giambra's autobiography, *The Uncrowned Champion*, written with Fred Villani, is what the fighter said to Sugar Ray Robinson and Bobo Olson before their August 26, 1955, championship fight at the Chicago Stadium.

Several months prior to their battle, Olson won an unpopular ten round decision over Giambra in which, the authors tell us, "bottles were thrown, fights broke out…and the Cow Palace became a mad house."

Before the Robinson-Olson fight began, Giambra was introduced to the crowd. After acknowledging the cheers, he grabbed the microphone and announced that "I'm Joey Giambra, the uncrowned champ."

First, he went to Robinson's corner and said to him, "Good luck, Sugar. Maybe if you win the title, I'll get a shot at you." Then he trotted to Olson's corner and said, "I'm pulling for you, Bobo. Beat this guy because I want another shot at you."

Olson's response—"Don't worry, Joey. If I win you got it"—surprised Giambra, who thought, *'If I win.' He sure didn't sound very confident."*

NO ONE EVER SEES BOB COMING

ob Saginowski is a shy, quiet bartender who works at Cousin Marv's Bar, and Eric Deeds is a quietly menacing vicious psychopath well-known to local authorities. They're two of the main characters in Dennis Lehane's novella *The Drop* (2014).

The setting is South Boston in 2009, and early on Bob rescues an abused dog belonging to Deeds, who tells him he can keep the dog for $10,000. He believes Bob can steal the money from Cousin Marv's Bar, which, Bob knows, is a wacky idea.

If Bob doesn't get the money, Deeds says, he'll take the dog back and continue abusing it.

One afternoon Deeds visits Bob at his home, demands the $10,000, and, before leaving, in an I'll-show-you-who's-boss move, takes Bob's umbrella. The next day Bob confronts Deeds outside his home.

> DEEDS: I'm not greedy, Bob. I just need stake money for
>   something. I don't want everything in the safe, just ten
>   grand. You give me ten grand, I'll disappear.
> BOB: This is ridiculous.
> DEEDS: So, it's ridiculous.
> BOB: You just don't walk into someone's life and—
> DEEDS: That *is* life—someone like me coming along when

you're not looking and you're not ready. I'm a hundred and seventy pounds worth of End Times, Bob.

Lehane, who also wrote the screenplay for the excellent 2014 movie of the same title, has created in Eric Deeds the personification of existential dread that sooner or later enters everyone's life unexpectedly and causes damage, physically and/or mentally.

Bob realizes that when a force like Deeds enters a person's life, it's as if, Lehane writes, "something in the fabric of the world has just been torn." But there are some individuals who retaliate when someone like Deeds appears and pushes them too far. Bob is one such individual, and he does what he has to do to make Deeds disappear.

And was he justified in doing what he did to Deeds? An unequivocal yes.

Aware of Deeds and the danger he possesses, veteran police detective Evandro Torres, his instinct working overtime, at the end of the novella visits Bob one morning at Cousin Marv's Bar.

His instinct tells him Bob has something to do with Deeds' disappearance, and if he does, well, that's okay. One less miscreant to deal with.

After some friendly small talk, Torres looks directly at Bob, and in the book's most significant line, admiringly says to him, "No one ever sees you coming, do they?"

A TOUCH OF FILM NOIR

THE ELM CITY

The Whalley Theater in New Haven is where I spent many summer afternoons as a curious, self-proclaimed legendary teen, watching first a B flick, usually from Allied Artists or Republic Pictures, then a main feature, usually from Warner Bros., MGM, Paramount, or 20th Century Fox.

Before the B movie began, there were previews of coming attractions, maybe a *Pete Smith Special*, two or three cartoons, and a newsreel.

I'd arrive at one o'clock in the afternoon, find a seat close to the screen, and almost four hours later, I'd leave the theater and head for home almost a mile away. (The moment I left the theater… oh, that bright sun.)

Many of those B movies were what later would be called film noir. Their heyday was in the 1940s and early 1950s. Ninety minutes. Filmed in black and white. Sometimes corny. Sometimes not.

Indeed, time has been kind to film noir: today they're written about and studied in colleges, praised by director Martin Scorsese, and even imitated (usually without success).

Film noir scholar Eddie Muller writes books about them.

CHARACTERISTICS

FOR STARTERS, TIME IN A FILM NOIR IS OFTEN SHATTERED. That is, the present is interrupted by a flashback, which means the past is always present. No one in a film noir escapes his or her past.

Narration. Don't be surprised that in a film noir you encounter voice-over narration. But watch out: it may not be conventional. Consider Billy Wilder's *Sunset Boulevard* (1950). As Julie Kirko writes in *Film Noir: An Encyclopedic Reference to the American Style*, "It is the rare film that declares itself immediately as does *Sunset Boulevard*. [It opens] with the sardonic narration of a dead man commenting mordantly on the circumstances of his own murder" and is "a strange kind of film noir."

Background. It's usually a city that provides the setting for film noir.

Space. It's tightened to create a sense of claustrophobia.

The Camera. High, off-center, and low angle camera shots are common, and the human face and body are often distorted, creating a sense of menace, of imbalance.

Shadows. Any respectable film noir must have shadows lurking—they're almost alive—on walls, hinting of a character's doom.

Venetian blinds. That's right: Venetian blinds. They fracture sunlight, or hope, and foreshadow and underline a character's doom.

Nighttime. A film noir usually takes place at night after a hard rain, the streets wet and slick.

Regarding the main characters in a film noir, Eddie Muller, in *Dark City: The Lost World of Film Noir*, says there are usually six: the sleuth, the criminal, the victim, the returning GI, the recently released prisoner, and the *femme fatale*.

Add, too, an atmosphere of steaminess in a good film noir.

FACES OF FILM NOIR

THE MOST CONVINCING AND SCARY FILM NOIR TEMPTRESS is Jane Greer as Kathy Moffet in 1947's *Out of the Past*, which Jacques Tourneur directed. (You have to ask yourself as you watch this movie, how can someone so gorgeous be so evil?)

Eddie Muller is spot on when he describes Greer as possessing "a beguiling trace of baby fat, a vestige of innocence, eyes sparkling with delight, a voice that had a smoky, nimble way with lies."

Witness Kathie's reaction as Jeff Markham (Robert Mitchum, no stranger to the film noir genre early in his movie career) and his former detective partner, the smarmy Jack Fisher (film noir stalwart Steve Brodie) slug it out in her bungalow. We hear a gunshot and Fisher falls to the floor, shot by Kathie.

Markham's expression is one of shock and disbelief, but Kathie is calm and smiling. She enjoyed the fight. She enjoyed killing Jack.

Richard Conte is the male face of film noir, especially for his performance as Mr. Brown, a vicious, impeccably attired gangster in Joseph H. Lewis' *The Big Combo* (1955).

For example, when Mr. Brown captures Cornel Wilde's police detective Leonard Diamond, he removes the hearing aid from his yes-man and one-time boss McClure (Brian Donlevy), places it in Diamond's ear, and shouts into the receiver. Diamond writhes in pain. Then he gives the receiver to one of his minions, who screams into it. Finally, he places it in front of a radio and turns up the volume. Diamond passes out.

At the end of the movie, Mr. Brown gets his long overdue comeuppance. The scene takes place in an airplane hangar, and Diamond, who has captured him, stands over the gangster, who seems to have shrunk and is now a small, defeated man.

LISTEN UP! MEL BROOKS HAS SIX FINGERS!

. . . For the most part to characterize my humor as purely Jewish humor is not accurate. It's really New York humor. New York humor is not just Jewish humor. It has a certain rhythm. It has a certain intensity and a certain pulse. Lenny Bruce, Rodney Dangerfield, Jackie Mason, and stand-up comedians like me were not simply Jewish. We were New York—there is a big difference.

—Mel Brooks, quoted in *All About Me!*

SIX FINGERS

All About Me! is Mel Brooks' wonderful memoir that proves Roger Ebert was spot on when he wrote that "[Brooks] will do anything for a laugh. Anything. He's an anarchist; his movies inhabit a universe in which everything is possible and the outrageous is probable..."

That said, what's the skinny about Brooks' six fingers?

Well, in 2018, Brooks was scheduled to have his handprints stamped into the sidewalk in front of Grauman's Chinese Theater on Hollywood Boulevard.

He admits he hadn't been involved in any mischievous behavior for a while, and it was time to change that. "I arranged to have the prop masters from *The Walking Dead* TV series build me a sixth finger on my left hand," he writes. "I wanted one of the hundreds of tourists that would visit the Chinese Theater sidewalk that day to shout, 'Hey! Did you know that Mel Brooks had SIX fingers on his left hand!'"

Don't stop there, Mel, who was born Melvin Kaminski in Brooklyn in 1926: "We pulled it off, and the prosthetic looked so real that I decided to wear my sixth finger on Conan O'Brien's show that same night. Nobody from his production team told Conan about it, so that when I revealed it in the middle of our interview, he went absolutely bananas!"

INSPECTOR KEMP

BROOKS ASSEMBLED A REMARKABLE CAST OF TALENTED ACTORS for 1974's *Young Frankenstein*: Peter Boyle as the monster, Gene Wilder as Dr. Frederick Frankenstein, Teri Garr as Inga, Cloris Leachman as Frau Blucher, Madeline Kahn as Elizabeth, Marty Feldman as Igor, Richard Hadyn as Herr Falkstein, an unbilled Gene Hackman as the blind hermit, and Kenneth Mars as Police Inspector Kemp.

Yes, yes, yes, the hugely talented Kenneth Mars as Kemp because, as Brooks writes, "any time I needed a crazy German, I knew I could count on Kenny Mars to be there. He came up with a wonderful suggestion: he would put his character's monocle over his black eye patch, thereby making it completely useless."

Kemp! He's my favorite character in *Young Frankenstein* because everything he does is hilarious.

There's his weird accent—which I won't describe because I can't.

There's the riot scene. To the excited villagers who have assembled one evening in front of police headquarters—they're protesting the arrival of another Frankenstein—Kemp says, after adjusting his wooden arm, which has a life of its own, "A riot is an ugly thing. But I think it's just about time we had one."

Inspired, the villagers cheer.

Then Kemp says that Frederick Frankenstein "will curse the day that he was born a Frankenstein."

But the villagers don't understand what he said and respond with a loud "WHAT!"

Slowly and clearly Kemp repeats what he said: "I said he will curse the day he was born a Frankenstein." The villagers cheer louder than before and are ready to riot.

Let's backtrack to the first time Kemp and Dr. Frankenstein meet. It occurs in the Frankenstein castle. While they're chatting, the doctor and the always suspicious Kemp begin throwing darts.

Talk and throw. Throw and talk.

It shouldn't be a surprise that when Dr. Frankenstein isn't looking, Kemp does some serious dart cheating.

Because they've been agitating each other, their aim has been affected: Darts are flying everywhere and missing the dart board.

One gets stuck in a lampshade.

Another breaks a window.

Another strikes the family cat. (MEOW! Poor cat.)

CLORIS THE GREAT

HERE'S WHAT BROOKS SAYS IS ONE OF HIS FAVORITE MOMENTS in *Young Frankenstein*. It occurs after music had been "emanating from the bowels of the castle," and Dr. Frankenstein, Inga, and Igor discover it "was played on the violin by none other than Frau Blucher."

FREDERICK: You played that music in the middle of the
   night!

FRAU BLUCHER: Yes!

FREDERICK:…to get us into the laboratory!

FRAU BLUCHER: Yes!

FREDERICK: That was your cigar smoldering in the ashtray!

FRAU BLUCHER: Yes!

FREDERICK: And it was you who left my grandfather's book out for me to find!

FRAU BLUCHER: Yes!

FREDERICK: So that I would…

FRAU BLUCHER: Yes!

FREDERICK: Then you and Victor were…

FRAU BLUCHER: YES! YES! SAY IT!…HE VAS MY BOYFRIEND!

As Frau Blucher the incredibly talented Cloris Leachman is, like her Nurse Diesel character in Brooks' *High Anxiety* (1977), unforgettably wacky.

And who can forget one of her most famous lines in 1977's *High Anxiety*? It occurs when she issues a warning to the staff of the Psycho-Neurotic Institute for the Very Very Nervous about being late for a meal.

With calculated wickedness, she says, "Those who are tardy do not get fruit cup." (And she means it!)

Priceless is the way to describe Leachman's unforgettable performances in those two movies.

And don't be late for a meal, especially if you want a fruit cup!

NICOL WILLIAMSON'S MAGIC SKULLCAP

Excalibur is more than a sword…for I believe it possesses magical powers and dignity and wonder and can't be separated from King Arthur's fate and Camelot.

—N. Gronsky, quoted in *The Book of Excalibur*

IT MUST BE MAGIC

I saw *Excalibur* for the first time in 1981.

After my second viewing three weeks ago, I did some research about Nicol Williamson, the movie's Merlin the Magician, and learned of his adventure with a prop.

A prop? Yes, because initially Williamson didn't understand what made Merlin tick. Fortunately, the movie's costume designer made a skullcap for the actor, and the moment Williamson placed it on his head, as Gabriel Hershman writes in *Black Sheep: The Authorised Biography of Nicol Williamson,* "the whole character came to him."

Williamson, who wore the skullcap in every scene in which he appeared, told Hershman he had fun playing Merlin, and that

"I tried to make him a cross between my old English teacher... and a space traveler..."

THE CAST

THE MOVIE, BASED ON T. H. WHITE'S *THE SWORD IN THE STONE* and Thomas Malory's *Le Morte D'Arthur*, has an impressive cast, including Nigel Terry as Arthur, Helen Mirren as Morgana, Nicholas Clay as Lancelot, Gabriel Byrne as Uther Pendragon, Patrick Sewart as Leondegrance, Liam Neeson as Gawain, Cherie Lunghi as Guinevere, and Williamson as Merlin.

Ah, yes, Mirren, Byrne, Stewart, Neeson, and Williamson were all so young.

KING ARTHUR QUESTIONS MERLIN

JOHN BOORMAN DIRECTED AND COWROTE THE MOVIE'S screenplay, and he doesn't waste any time. *Excalibur*'s opening scene is all action. Led by Uther Pendragon, one of King Arthur's knights, we see bodies falling and blood flowing and we hear swords clanging.

Enter Merlin. Uther sees him and bellows, "Merlin, I am the strongest. I am the one. You promised me [Excalibur]," and Merlin says, "You shall have it, but to heal, not to hack."

It isn't what Williamson's Merlin says to Uther but how he says it and how he looks when he says it. As he speaks, there's a hint of a snarl.

Watch his eyes too: He acts with them.

Later in the movie, King Arthur, taking a break from feasting with his men, seeks an answer to a question about life, and who better to ask than Merlin, his trusted friend and advisor?

"What is the greatest quality of life? Courage? Passion? Loyalty? Humility? What do you say, Merlin?"

But before Merlin can respond, Arthur demands a straight answer from him, which is, "No poetry!"

Again, watch and listen to Merlin's reply: "All right, then. Truth, that's it. Yes. It must be truth above all. When a man lies, he murders some part of the world."

Later in the movie, King Arthur asks Merlin about evil.

KING ARTHUR: Then answer me this. Peace reigns in the land. Crops grow in abundance. There's no wont. Every one of my subjects enjoys his happiness and justice. Tell me, Merlin, have we defeated evil? It seems we have.
MERLIN: Good and evil cannot live without the other.
KING ARTHUR: Where hides evil, then, in my kingdom?
MERLIN: Always where you never expect it. Always.

Of course, Merlin has other insights. Near the end of the movie, King Arthur asks him if he's a dream, and he replies, "Sometimes I am a dream. Sometimes I'm a nightmare." Then he disappears.

A DIGRESSION ON THE GODFATHER MOVIE AND THEN BACK TO WILLIAMSON'S MERLIN

MARLON BRANDO REJUVENATED HIS CAREER WHEN HE WON the Oscar for 1972's Best Actor for his portrayal of Don Vito Corleone in *The Godfather*. Would his *Godfather* performance ever be surpassed?

Thirteen years later came *Prizzi's Honor* and William Hickey's turn as a wise, dying, and practical eighty-seven-year-old

Godfather named Don Corrado Prizzi. (Hickey was fifty-seven years old when he played Prizzi.)

Did Hickey's Godfather out-Brando Brando's? Yes! His voice is frightening, and he looks like a vampire in need of blood and ready to strike. Unsettling is the best way to describe him.

And don't dare think of crossing him, because all he has to do is snap his fingers and his minions will appear, and they'll do grievous harm to your person while he watches and chuckles.

I haven't seen many King Arthur movies, but for another actor to outdo Nicol Willimson's portrayal of Merlin, well, I don't see it happening. Williamson's Merlin is simply too fascinating to be surpassed or even equaled.

It isn't an exaggeration to say Williamson is one of those rare actors whose performances sometimes are too big for the big screen.

BILLY JOEL, MOZART, AND THE BEATLES

I will never run out of musical ideas, but I find sometimes that words, rather than enhancing music, can tend to limit it. I don't set out to write a song about anything; I want to write a piece of music that really moves me, and then I go, 'How do I interpret this lyrically?'

—Billy Joel

MOM AND DAD

BILLY JOEL HAS BEEN MAKING MUSIC SINCE THE 1970S AS A singer, pianist, and songwriter, and I confess I didn't pay much attention to his work. I took it for granted.

Enough said—except to say that in October 2022 for some odd reason after listening to him on the radio and watching him on YouTube, I began paying hard attention to his lyrics and the stories they tell and their various themes.

William Martin Joel was born on May 9, 1949, in the Bronx, New York, and shortly after his birth, he and his family moved to Levittown, New York.

Though his father Howard, a German immigrant, was a classically trained pianist, it was his mother Rosalind who encouraged Billy, when he was four years old, to play the piano.

His father "thought [pop music] was crap," Joel told Timothy White in "A Portrait of the Artist." "Popular music for him stopped when he got to the big band era. He respected jazz guys like Erroll Garner, who he thought was tops, and he had kind words for Nat King Cole, but nobody after that."

RINGO AND THE OTHERS

JOEL SAID HIS BIGGEST INFLUENCES WERE "BEETHOVEN, Mozart, Chopin, Debussy," but "…the single biggest moment I can remember being galvanized into wanting to be a musician was seeing the Beatles on *The Ed Sullivan Show*.

"John F. Kennedy had been assassinated in November of 1963, and the country was in a funk….The country really had the blues, [and] during the civil rights movement a lot of radio would not play rhythm and blues like Jackie Wilson, Otis Redding, Wilson Pickett, James Brown….So they tried to pretty it up. They came out with Frankie Avalon, Fabian, Bobby Rydell, and all these boring bullshit guys, and all of a sudden there's this band with hair like girls…and they played their own instruments and they wrote their own songs, and they didn't look like Fabian. They looked like kids…we all knew,…and I said at that moment that's what I want to do. I want to be like those guys."

SOME BILLY FACTS

- He dropped out of high school to pursue his musical career.
- His breakthrough hit was "The Stranger" (1977).

- The 1980s were his biggest years, with such hits as "Uptown Girl," Tell Her About It," "Innocent Man," and "The Longest Time."
- In 1989, he was presented with the Grammy Legend Award.
- In 1999, he was inducted into the Rock and Roll Hall of Fame.
- In the early 2000s, he was in and out of rehab, struggling with alcohol addiction.
- In 2013, he was honored by the Kennedy Center for Performing Arts.
- His third wife, Alexis Roderick, gave birth to a baby girl, Della Rose, in 2015.

SONGS

Many of Joel's songs are nostalgia themed. For example, there's 1986's "Time to Remember," with its gentle warning not to take time for granted: "This is the time to remember/'Cause it will not last forever/These are the days/To hold on to/'Cause we won't/Although we want to."

In 2002's "Scenes from an Italian Restaurant," one of his longest, most involved pieces, we learn that "Brenda and Eddie were the popular steadies/And the king and queen at the prom/…Nobody looked any finer/Or was more of a hit at the parkway diner/We never knew we could want more than that out of life/Surely Brenda and Eddie would always know how to survive."

One wonders if, in Billy Joel's world, Brenda and Eddie survived, but what we know for certain is they "started to fight when the money got tight/…The best they could do was pick up the pieces/Can't tell you anymore/… And here we are waving Brenda and Eddie goodbye."

WHAT STANDS OUT FOR ME (2)

In Nicholas Meyer's *The Seven-Per-cent Solution: Being a Reprint from the Reminiscences of John H. Watson, M.D.* (1974) is Sherlock Holmes' first meeting with Sigmund Freud at the physician's Vienna home.

Holmes and Watson, the master detective's friend and biographer, have traveled to Vienna hoping Freud would find the cause of and perhaps cure Holmes' cocaine addiction, why he is obsessed with Professor Moriarty, and why he distrusts women.

Holmes and Watson meet Freud, and before long the doctor samples the detective's powers of observation. For example, "You are married, possess a sense of humor," Holmes says to Freud, "and enjoy playing cards and reading Shakespeare and a Russian author whose name I am unable to pronounce."

Holmes continues: "That you are a physician is clear to me when I glance at your medical degree on the far wall. That you no longer practice medicine is evident by your presence here at home in the middle of the day, with no apparent anxiety on your part about a schedule to keep. Your separation from various societies is indicated by those spaces on the wall, clearly meant to display additional certificates. The color of the paint there is somewhat paler in small rectangles, and an outline of dust shows me where they used to be."

Holmes isn't shy about showboating his powers of observation and deduction, is he? Freud isn't intimidated, however, and is thrilled by his guest's observations, exclaiming that "this is wonderful!"

…is the last scene in 1983's *Tootsie*, but, first, consider Dustin Hoffman's Michael Dorsey, an unemployed actor who became employed after he disguised himself as a middle-aged woman named Dorothy Michaels and appeared on a trashy TV show and audiences loved her, and the show soared in the ratings, reaching number one in the country, and I'll stop here to take a breath.

Final scene: Dorsey is in love with Julie Nichols (Jessica Lange), but she's angry at him because she thought he was a she, not a he. Dorsey tells her that "I just did it for the work. I didn't mean to hurt anybody, especially you….Look, you don't know me from Adam, but I was a better man with you as a woman than I ever was with a woman as a man. Know what I mean?"

(I hope I got that right…)

It's Michael Dorsey's most honest and insightful moment, revealing how much he has grown and learned about life from his *life* as a woman.

ONE OF THE BEST

If you had to define professional boxing in the 1980s, with just ten fighters, Marlon Starling's name was a must....There are some who don't remember that both professional and amateur boxing was outlawed in 1965 by an act of the Connecticut State General Assembly. The unconscionable decree immediately shelved the future of half a generation of potential ring stars from the state of Connecticut. Marlon Starling was the fighter who brought it back.

—Mark Allen Baker, author and boxing historian

MAGIC MAN

Hartford-born Marlon Starling won twenty-five consecutive fights before suffering a split decision loss to Donald Curry in 1984. At stake were the World Boxing Association welterweight title and the International Boxing Federation welterweight title.

Prior to Starling's loss to Curry, in 1983 he had defeated Kevin Howard at the Hartford Civic Center to win the North American Boxing Federation and the United States Boxing Association welterweight titles.

That same year he successfully defended his titles against

Tommy Ayers, this time in Las Vegas at the Showboat Hotel & Casino, Sports Pavilion.

In 1985, he outpointed Floyd Mayweather Sr. in Atlantic City to win the USBA Welterweight Championship.

Two years later, Starling, nicknamed "Magic Man," faced undefeated World Boxing Association welterweight champion Mark Breland. The fight took place at the Township Auditorium in South Carolina, and Starling worked his magic that night, recording a sensational come-from-behind TKO in the eleventh round.

A huge favorite, the lanky Breland, a talented fighter known for his punching power, boxing acumen, and stinging left jab, was leading on the officials' scorecards (99-91, 99-89, and 97-92) going into round eleven.

The well-conditioned, determined Starling was getting stronger as the fight progressed, while Breland appeared to be tiring.

With two minutes remaining in the eleventh round, Magic Man hurt Breland with a barrage of punches and then knocked him down with a devastating left hook to the head.

Though Breland managed to beat the count, he was in no condition to continue, and referee Tony Perez stopped the fight.

Hartford's Marlon Starling was the new WBA welterweight champion!

Boxing historian Mark Allen Baker, the author of eight books about boxing, writes that "as boxing fans know, Breland had an incredible amateur career" of 110-1, with seventy-three knockouts. "For Marlon Starling to defeat Breland, in [Breland's] first WBA Welterweight Championship defense, was really an extraordinary accomplishment."

In Starling's first title defense—1988 was the year—he won a unanimous decision over Fujio Ozaki in Atlantic City's Convention Center.

The rematch with Breland took place in Las Vegas, also in

1988, and ended in a draw, which meant Starling had retained his WBA championship.

Not everyone agreed with the decision: HBO judge and analyst Harold Lederman said that "I saw it 8-4, in favor of Moochie Starling….The fight was marred by a lot of holding and grabbing, pushing and shoving. But Moochie landed the harder, cleaner, and more effective punches and was in control….I think Moochie retained the title that night, and I think he did a darn good job."

Three months after the second Breland fight, Starling defended his WBA title against undefeated Tomas Molinares in Atlantic City's Conventional Hall. The fight had a chaotic ending: Though an overhand right by Molinares knocked Starling out, it was clearly delivered at least two seconds after the bell rang ending round six.

"…One of the luckiest punches of all time," said HBO blow-by-blow commentor Jim Lampley, "and in my view clearly after the bell."

Later, the fight was declared no contest.

In 1989, Starling became the World Boxing Council world welterweight champion by stopping England's Lloyd Honeyghan in Las Vegas.

That same year, at Hartford's Civic Center, he defended his WBC title against Young Kil Jung, winning a unanimous decision.

In 1990, in Las Vegas, undefeated Michael Nunn outpointed Starling in the latter's bid for the International Boxing Federation world middleweight championship.

Four months later Starling fought Maurice Blocker in Reno, Nevada, and lost his WBC welterweight title by decision.

One of the best defensive and savviest fighters of his time, Starling began boxing professionally in 1979 and retired in 1990 with an impressive 45-6-1 (1 NC) record.

Could he punch? Yes! Twenty-seven of his wins were by KO. Could he take a punch? Yes! During his long career, he was never legitimately stopped.

In 2005, he was inducted into the Connecticut Boxing Hall of Fame.

WBA, WBC, USBA, NABF, WCC, even HBO…Man, oh man, I hope I got all those organizations correct, though I'm suspicious of HBO.

AN APPLE, A CHAIR, AND A CAT

SNATCHES

Elisa Gabbert is spot on when she writes, in a recent *New York Times Book Review* column, of a friend whose "favorite way to read poetry is in quotation, as isolated lines in paragraphs of prose. I've come to many poems I love in similar ways. . . .I think poetry is best caught in snatches. . ."

Gabbert quotes the following fragment of poetry from Nobel Prize winner Pablo Neruda's "Ode to the Apple": "When we bite into/your round innocence/we too regress/for a moment/to the state/of the newborn:/there's still some apple in us all."

. . .still some apple in us all.

Ferris Cook selected twenty-five of Neruda's odes, along with illustrating the poet's wonderful *Odes to Common Things*, a volume honoring things we take for granted, such as a spoon, an orange, bread, an onion, and French fries.

(I've always liked odes because they often praise something or someone.)

Here's a bit from Neruda's "Ode to the Chair": "War is as vast as the shadowy jungle./A single chair/ is the first sign/of/ peace."

A stunning insight and image.

NARRATIVE

Story poems? Love them, too, because they have a narrative.

In American poet Thomas Lynch's "Grimalkin," from his book *Bone Cemetery*, the poem's main character is its narrator, Lynch himself, and as the poem progresses he tells us about his son Mike and the family cat Grimalkin, whom—or maybe it's who—the twelve-year-old loves intensely.

Writes Lynch: "And under Mike's protection she will fix her/ indolent green-eyed gaze on me/as if to say: Whaddaya gonna do about it, Slick,/the child loves me and you love the child."

Grimalkin has driven Lynch wacky from the moment she became a member of his family. No surprise that he regularly thinks that "…one of these days she will lie there and be dead./And choking back loud hallelujahs, I'll pretend/a brief bereavement for Michael's sake,/letting him think as he has often said/deep down inside you really love her don't you Dad."

What Lynch writes in the final lines of his poem about his son—that "all boys need practice in the arts of love"—is admirable, but what he says about himself—that "all boys' aging fathers [need practice] in the arts of rage"— is questionable. (I mean: rage over a cat.)

Wait! I know what Mr. Lynch's problem is: He doesn't have any apple in him.

HOLMES IS RECOVERING

In 1891, Sherlock Holmes was missing and presumed dead for three years. This is a true story of that disappearance. Only the facts have been made up.

—Nicholas Meyer, quoted in *The Seven-Per-Cent Solution*

WHAT NICOL WILLIAMSON, WHO WAS BORN IN HAMILTON, WHICH IS NEAR GLASGOW, SAID ABOUT HIS PERFORMANCE AS HOLMES AND DOYLE

"I have never seen a Holmes movie, nor read any of Conan Doyle's stories, and neither do I intend to do so. Everyone has had a go at playing Holmes, but my Holmes is different. The man is in the grip of a terrible affliction. The man is in a state of collapse. He's serious but with a slight dash of humor, not just a hat and a pipe."

AN ALL-STAR CAST

THE SEVEN-PER-CENT SOLUTION'S ALL-STAR CAST STARS ALAN Arkin as Dr. Sigmund Freud, Robert Duvall as Dr. John Watson, Sir Laurence Olivier as Professor James Moriarty, Vanessa Redgrave as Lola Devereaux, Joel Grey as Lowenstein, and Williamson as a deeply troubled Sherlock Holmes.

Herbert Ross directed and Nicholas Meyer, who penned the 1974 novel of the same title, wrote the screenplay.

The entertaining, fast-paced 1976 movie involves Holmes and his friend and biographer Watson traveling to Vienna to meet Dr. Sigmund Freud. Their hope is that he will help the master detective recover from his cocaine addiction, from his obsession with Professor Moriarty, and from his distrust of women.

(Oh, those snakes that populate Holmes' deep-seated cocaine-induced hallucinations! Run for cover.)

In Vienna, the level-headed Freud tells Watson he intends to hypnotize Holmes, then enter his consciousness so he'll confront the horrific childhood event that caused his cocaine addiction and his other problems.

HOLMES (MILDLY) REPRIMANDS DR. FREUD

EARLY IN *THE SEVEN-PER-CENT SOLUTION*, HOLMES HAS MUCH to say to Freud and Watson about a stranger seated near them as they dine in a restaurant.

Freud, always curious, asks how Holmes knows so much about the man.

Staring directly at Freud, Holmes replies, "You see but you do not observe," adding that it's a "faculty" that you must embrace and develop, which is what Freud will do.

HOLMES' OBSESSION WITH MORIARTY AND THE MOVIE'S BIG REVEAL

UNDER HYPNOSIS, WE LEARN THE REASON WHY HOLMES HAS been obsessed with the professor for so long.

FREUD: Why did you become a detective?
HOLMES: To punish the wicked and see justice done.
FREUD: Have you ever known wickedness personally? Have you?
HOLMES: Yes.
FREUD: What was this wickedness?
HOLMES: My mother deceived my father.
FREUD: She had a lover?
HOLMES: Yes.
FREUD: And what was the injustice? What was the injustice?
HOLMES: He shot her.
FREUD: Your father murdered your mother?
HOLMES: Yes.
FREUD: And the lover? What became of him? Who was he? (Emphatically) Who was he?
HOLMES: My tutor.
FREUD: Professor Moriarty?
HOLMES: Yes. Professor Moriarty.
FREUD: (Pause) All right, sleep now. Sleep. Remember nothing. You understand? You will remember nothing.

To Watson, Freud points out that "it becomes clear how much is observed by these facts. We understand not only the origin of his fixation and his hatred for Professor Moriarty, but also his suspicion of women and…also his choice of profession. Detector of wickedness, punisher of injustice."

A grateful Watson responds by telling Freud that "you're the greatest detective of them all," and the renowned psychiatrist modestly replies that "I am a physician whose province is the troubled mind, which means in this case I have simply borrowed some of your friend's techniques and applied them to himself. You will remember we spoke of an area of the mind called the unconscious, and he has led me to it. He has given me the clues himself."

At the end of the movie, thanks to Freud, Holmes is on the road to recovery because—and this is key to the master detective's recovery—he's no longer in denial about the horrific incident in his childhood involving his parents and Professor Moriarty.

BON VOYAGE AND HELLO, LOLA

THE MOVIE ENDS WITH HOLMES LEAVING LONDON BY SHIP, and he won't say where he's going because, he tells Watson, "I need some time to myself....Take a holiday."

"When will you return?" Watson asks.

"Oh, one day....My dear fellow, it's only that I must complete my recovery."

Though the heart of the movie concerns the reason *why* Holmes became addicted to cocaine and his other emotional problems, there's also a kidnapping plot that might have international repercussions in which Holmes becomes involved. Redgrave's Lola Deveraux was the victim.

On the ship's deck, Holmes recognizes the lady seated next to him is Lola, and they engage in friendly conversation. It soon becomes obvious they're attracted to each other.

The Holmes we see in this scene is happy and relaxed because he's in recovery. As for returning to London, I read somewhere he'll be back in probably three years.

(ALMOST) EVERYTHING YOU SHOULD KNOW ABOUT NICOL WILLIAMSON

—Paul Moriarty, quoted in
Martin Dowsing's *Beware the Actor.*

—Martin Dowsing, quoted in *Beware the Actor*

NIXON'S WHITE HOUSE

IF YOU'VE READ MARTIN DOWSING'S SUPERB BIOGRAPHY OF the late Nicol Williamson, *Beware the Actor: The Rise and Fall of Nicol Williamson*, you'll recall that on March 19, 1970, Williamson became the first actor invited to perform at the White House.

He appeared in a one-hour, one man performance before President Richard Nixon and close to three hundred guests.

Nixon had learned about Williamson from Prime Minister Harold Wilson, who told him the actor was Great Britain's greatest stage actor and "the best Hamlet in a generation and perhaps of the century..."

The president's curiosity was piqued, and arrangements were made for Williamson to perform at the White House. His program consisted of readings from Shakespeare, T. S. Eliot, and Samuel Beckett, and he was backed by a nine-member band called the World's Greatest Jazz Band.

The show was "very well received and all the critics present gave rave reviews," Dowsing writes. Initially Williamson believed "it had gone well," but later in a *Penthouse* interview said that "'It stank.'"

NICOL AND THE STUDENTS

A MATINEE PERFORMANCE OF *MACBETH* AT THE ROYAL Shakespeare Theater, Stratford-upon-Avon for high school students...The date: December 4, 1974...Williamson played Macbeth.

Jane Lapotaire, a Tony Award winner for her 1978 performance as Edith Piaf in *Piaf* on Broadway, was cast as the second witch, Lady Macduff, and as Banquo's son Fleance.

During the performance, she remembers the scene when Macbeth says, "Is this a dagger I see before me,/The handle toward my hand? Come let me clutch thee. /I have thee not, and yet I see thee still./Art thou not, fatal vision, sensible/To feeling as to sight? Or art thou but/a dagger of the mind, a false creation/Proceeding from the heat-oppressed brain?"

Then, says Laportaire, "[Nicol] took the stool out from under him and threw it though the space where he saw the dagger. Brilliant idea."

To Williamson's chagrin, the students in the audience "thought [it] was the funniest thing they ever saw" and began laughing.

What he did next was stop the play. Then, according to Lapotaire, he "walked to the front of the stage and said something along the lines of, 'Surprising though it may seem to some of you, there are people in this theater that want to hear this play. Those of you who don't, leave now.'

"Nobody left, and the audience remained silent for the rest of the play," Lapotaire says. "While this incident is often cited as an example of Nicol's difficult behaviour, the schoolchildren had apparently been noisy and disruptive from the beginning, but many in the audience must have been grateful that someone had finally given them a proper reprimand."

CHUTZPAH?

THE ALDWYCH THEATER, LONDON, ENGLAND, 1975. WILliamson, once again playing the title character in Shakespeare's *Macbeth*, and Paul Moriarty, his understudy, were drinking at the Opera Theater, located near the Aldwych.

According to Martin Dowsing, Paul Moriarty said that "after three pints, it was nearly a quarter past seven. We went back, and he put in forty minutes on the play that night. I was playing Lennox…and he lurched from scene to scene, virtually, but he got through it….He got right to the end and he said, 'Tomorrow and tomorrow and tomorrow…' and his face went white."

"Then Williamson paused, as only he can pause, looked out at the audience, and said, 'You all know the line—what is it?' And somebody in the audience shouted out, 'Creeps in this petty pace!' Williamson said, 'Thank you.' It was the first time I'd seen an actor blow that part…."

Blow that part!…Could it be that Williamson faked forgetting his lines and then asked for help because it got the audience involved? After all, he loved being unpredictable and was witty enough to try such a stunt.

As for the next night's performance, Paul Moriarty said that "Williamson did the tomorrow and tomorrow scene without a problem" and "it wasn't alluded to again."

COX'S HANNIBAL LECTER

[The purpose of an actor is to] touch on the inner life of people, what they are, where their disappointments are, where their love is, where their desire is, what they're seeking, and we become conduits for it.

> —Brian Cox, quoted in *Putting the Rabbit in the Hat*

[Cox's book is indeed] a meditation on craft and a paean to acting....

> —Quoted in *The New Yorker*

HOPKINS DID IT HIS WAY

OF FOREMOST INTEREST IN BRIAN COX'S EXCELLENT MEMOIR, *Putting the Rabbit in the Hat*, is the difference between Cox's interpretation of Hannibal Lecter in 1986's *Manhunter*, which Michael Mann directed, and Anthony Hopkins' take on the same character in director Jonathan Demme's 1991 *Silence of the Lambs*.

Born in 1946, in Dundee, Scotland, Cox, a distinguished Shakespearean actor, writes that "Hopkins' Lecter was genuinely frightening. You wouldn't turn your back on him, while [mine] was intellectual...very, very clever...."

Cox adds that if you saw his Lecter "on the street, you wouldn't look twice at him. He wouldn't stand out for his manners…or some kind of exaggerated charisma. He's just an ordinary looking, sounding, and acting guy who happens to have a razor-sharp brain." (And, er, a penchant for killing and eating people.)

Cox wasn't hired to play Lecter in *The Silence of the Lambs* because Jonathan Demme "wanted to do everything in a fresh and original way, and he wasn't interested in who played Hannibal first. Directors are like that."

INSTRUMENT

ONE OF COX'S MOST MEMORABLE EXPERIENCES AS A STAGE and film actor occurred in 1991: He and several other actors performed Shakespeare's *King Lear* at Broadmoor, a psychiatric institute for men and women.

Cox, who portrayed Lear, says that "I was taken aback by the fact that whenever a sword was drawn during the play, every member of the audience would look down, and when the sword was away again, they would look up.

"I had the line," he continues, "'Is there any cause in nature for these hard facts?' and there was a young woman sitting in the front row who suddenly moaned in—what?—pain? Recognition?"

Later he learned the woman "rarely spoke, and she was inside for attacking her sister….There physically, actually in the flesh, was that process of guilt being worked out within her. Yes, that word again. Expiation….She wasn't the only one who got something out of it. This was no group of bored schoolkids, forced to submit to a bit of culture or face the consequences. These guys, men and women, the inmates of a high-security psychiatric prison, came of their own free will…."

What the inmates did was "[allow] themselves to become totally involved."

Those are the moments, Cox adds, that are "incredible" and "make the job worthwhile....There are times when you see yourself as an instrument."

THE RISE, FALL, AND RISE OF AARON PRYOR

But don't you worry about "The Hawk." The ol' Hawk will fly again, just real low this time around!!!

—Aaron Pryor, quoted in The Flight of the Hawk: The Aaron Pryor Story

[Aaron Pryor] went from the bottom of the world right to the top…and couldn't handle the money, and he couldn't handle the pressures of being [the junior welterweight] champion.

—Ken Hawk, quoted in The Flight of the Hawk: The Aaron Pryor Story

THE LOSS

NICKNAMED "THE HAWK," CINCINNATI'S AARON PRYOR HAD forty professional fights, scored thirty-five KOs, and was defeated only once before retiring in 1990.

Pryor's one loss took place in 1987 at the Sunrise Musical Theater in Sunrise, Florida, against Bobby Joe Young of Steubenville,

Ohio. Pryor writes about the fight in the "Up in Smoke" chapter of his stunning autobiography *Flight of the Hawk: The Aaron Pryor Story* (1996/Book World, Inc), cowritten with Marshall Terrill.

Young tagged him in round seven with "a blow to my ear that dropped me," Pryor writes. "I rose to my feet, but for some strange reason, I kept my back to the referee" who was "baffled by my actions and kept counting."

Things become even stranger when "I genuflected and made a gesture to the cross, very much like a Catholic would when entering church; however, I wasn't a Catholic. I can only chalk it up to my drug-induced state," though that "didn't stop referee Bernie Soto from counting."

When Soto reached ten, he "ruled the fight a knockout" win for Young.

The fight was televised. It was probably the most surreal ending to a fight I ever saw. I never forgot it.

THE AUTOBIOGRAPHY

ON OCTOBER 19, 2016, AT AGE SIXTY-ONE, PRYOR DIED following a long battle with heart disease, but before his passing he was able to take charge of his self-destructive life and conquer his drug addiction.

His cautionary, bracingly honest autobiography takes you on a disturbing and unforgettable journey involving a talented but troubled junior world welterweight champion.

Chapter One, "Running on Empty," introduces the reader to Pryor's nightmarish childhood and to his mother Sara Shelery, a hard drinking, gun-toting woman with a violent temper.

Pryor writes that he "was the product of a one-night stand"; that he had seven siblings whose occupations "became drinking, drugging, stealing, robbing, and killing"; that of those children, five "had different fathers"; and that only his sister Barbara turned out to be "the steadiest of the Pryor clan."

When Pryor was eight years old, a Baptist minister sexually molested him, an incident that "robbed me of my spirituality for years," Pryor writes. "After the molestation, I couldn't be persuaded to set foot inside a church for another twenty years."

ADDICTION

PRYOR DISCUSSES HIS CRACK COCAINE ADDICTION IN "THE High Life" chapter and introduces us to the beautiful, sophisticated, and treacherous Theresa Adams, the woman who turned him on to crack.

She was six years Pryor's senior and, at the time, the love of his life. But in retrospect, Pryor realizes he was obsessed with her, an obsession so "blinding" that, he writes, "If she said jump, I asked, 'How high?'"

By the mid-1980s, Adams was almost unrecognizable. According to Pryor's former trainer Frankie Sims, "…her face was wrinkled and sunk in….This once beautiful goddess was reduced to this old-looking lady. I mean, I was terrified. I said to myself, 'So this is what crack will do to you?…'It was as if the evil that she had dealt to other people had finally caught up with her."

The chapter also contains Pryor's haunting image of his first crack house experience, which took place in Miami's Liberty City and was "where every street hustler, pimp, and prostitute seemed to gather. I also saw white men in business suits smoking rock, huddled up in the corner. Every race, every creed, every color was in that place. The addiction of crack breaks all social and racial barriers. It knows no prejudice."

DOMESTIC WOES

Pryor admits that he cheated on his first wife, Carol, with the predatory Adams.

His loyal friend Ken Hawk says it was Carol—and Pryor agrees with him—"who was the only woman who truly loved [him]. She was there for him before he won the championship. She was there for him when he was down and out after the Olympic Trials and he didn't have a cent to his name."

When he left Carol for Theresa, Hawk continues, he made one of the biggest mistakes of his life.

THE BIG FIGHT

The date was August 2, 1980, the place Cincinnati's Riverfront Coliseum, and Pryor fought WBA junior welterweight champion Antonio Cervantes and scored a fourth-round knockout.

One year later, Pryor would defend his WBA junior welterweight title against popular three-weight world champion Alexis Arguello.

In the chapter titled "Arguello 1," he writes about their classic first meeting on November 12, 1982, before twenty-four thousand fans in Miami's Orange Bowl.

"We were giving each other the best we had," Pryor writes.

In the fourteenth round, Pryor came on like a hurricane; after landing twenty-three unanswered punches to Arguello's face, referee Stanley Christodoulou stopped the fight.

Pryor had retained his WBA junior world welterweight title.

As most boxing fans know, after the fight a controversy erupted involving the contents of a black bottle Pryor drank from between rounds. Were its contents legal? Did it contain stimulants?

"Sorry to disappoint any conspiracy buffs," Pryor writes, "but it was just Peppermint Schnapps in the bottle. Peppermint Schnapps gives a fighter a cooling sensation in the mouth and feels as if you are inhaling more oxygen."

Frankie Sims believes the drink contained "the essence of peppermint…in a vial in liquid form. The ammonia opens the chest and nasal passages….The boxer still feels tired, but he no longer feels his chest on fire, and this is what Panama Lewis [Pryor's trainer] gave Aaron….It's legal, just not in a fight, [and] technically, if they would have found the water bottle, Arguello could have been awarded the fight….I've always told Aaron that Panama Lewis was no good for him. He did a lot of dirty things I didn't approve of."

On September 10, 1983, in their second bout, this time in Las Vegas, Pryor scored a tenth-round knockout to retain his junior welterweight title, which he held from 1980 to 1983.

From 1984 to 1985 he was the International Boxing Federation super lightweight title holder.

After retiring from boxing in 1996, Pryor was inducted into the International Boxing Hall of Fame. Three years later, the Associated Press voted him the number one junior welterweight of all time.

THE EPIPHANY

In "Redemption," Pryor is admitted to Bethesda Hospital in Montgomery, Ohio, suffering from bleeding ulcers. On an April Sunday in 1993, after spending three weeks in the hospital, he's released and makes his way to the New Friendship Church in Avondale, Ohio, pastored by Reverend A. L. Harvey.

And since that day, Pryor writes—it's the book's most significant line—"[I] have remained clean and sober…and I'm convinced that it was divine intervention that saved me…"

According to Ken Hawk, Pryor emerged from Bethesda Hospital a changed man. "I think he said to himself, 'I almost died, and I've got to change.' For the first time in his life, he was truly frightened."

Hawk believes his friend underwent "a spiritual awakening. That's when he'd seen the light. Thank God he saw something."

After his near-death experience, Pryor began teaching at-risk young people, mostly from Cincinnati, "about Christianity as well as drug addiction. I tell them what I tell anybody who hears me preach. The message I have for children contemplating smoking crack or freebasing cocaine is this: curiosity killed the cat, and it almost killed Aaron Pryor....Don't even give drugs a chance.... You smoke crack once, and you're addicted."

Pryor's work was so valuable to the community that he was ordained a deacon in Reverend Harvey's church on June 5, 1994. "They used to call me 'Champ,' he writes, "but now they call me 'Deacon.' I like it."

HE'S CALLED LITTLE JOHN

CALL ME MOTHER JENNET

What a cast! Directed by Richard Lester, *Robin and Marian* (1976) stars Sean Connery as Robin, Audrey Hepburn as Maid Marian, Ian Holm as King John, Richard Harris as Richard the Lionhearted, Robert Shaw as the Sheriff of Nottingham, and Nicol Williamson as Little John.

The movie involves the return from the Crusades to Sherwood Forest of Robin and Little John, who have been gone for twenty years. Middle-aged, tired, and battle-weary, Robin hopes to win back Lady Marian, the love of his life.

At the Abbey, they meet for the first time since Robin's return. Initially, he's taken aback by her appearance.

ROBIN: What are you doing in that costume?
MARIAN: Living in it.
ROBIN: I've come home to you, Marian. The wars are over. I'm here.
MARIAN: I'm Mother Jennet now. You can trot right back to Jerusalem.
ROBIN: You're angry.

MARIAN: Not with you. I haven't thought of you in twenty years.

(She doesn't tell him that after he left, she attempted suicide.)

IT'S OLD AGE

IN ONE OF HIS MOST PERCEPTIVE OBSERVATIONS ABOUT THE movie, Martin Dowsing writes, in his biography of Williamson, *Beware the Actor: The Rise and Fall of Nicol Williamson*, "It's very much an autumnal film, and the effects of age on the protagonists are subtly emphasized.

"We see Robin and his men waking up at night in the forest, joints stiff from the cold. After kneeling down to pray while wearing his armour, the Sheriff has difficulty getting back up again. Mounting a horse has become a struggle, and the fights are graceless and ungentlemanly....He and the Sheriff are trying to recapture their youth, but their ability is gone."

During the showdown near the end of the movie between Robin and the Sheriff, "the heaviness of the swords is emphasized," Dowsing writes, "and every swing of the blade is an effort punctuated by a grunt."

MARIAN AND LITTLE JOHN

ONE OF THE MOVIE'S MOST POIGNANT SCENES OCCURS ON the night Little John learns from Marian that Robin and the Sheriff will be engaging in a duel the next morning.

"He's mad," Little John says to Marian. "It's four-to-one against. We'll be slaughtered."

When Marian entreats Little John to tell Robin not to fight

the Sheriff, he says, "Say no to Rob? We've always been together. I'm nothing without him."

Most importantly, the scene reveals how Little John feels about Marian. "You're Rob's lady," he says. "If you were mine, I never would've left."

Hoping to assuage her distress, he tells her that "Robin will return."

The next morning, after a furious battle, Robin kills the Sheriff. As Little John helps his friend to his feet, the bloodied and wounded Robin playfully asks him, "You're a stout fellow. What are you called?"

Looking at Robin, he replies, "They call me Little John."

Perfect!

PERFORMANCE

WILLIAMSON PLAYS HIS CHARACTER IN A RESTRAINED, believable, and sincere manner, embodying what a proper friend should be.

Along with his unforgettable and fierce interpretation of Merlin in *Excalibur* and his unique take of Sherlock Holmes in *The Seven-Per-Cent Solution,* Little John is one of Williamson's best screen performances.

Regarding how the movie ends, you'll have mixed emotions.

THE BITE FIGHT

What a refreshing, informed point of view the late Katherine Dunn has about the sweet science!

In her exceptional *One Ring Circus: Dispatches from the World of Boxing* (2009), which is a compilation of her boxing writings from the *Portland Willamette Week*, *Vogue Magazine*, *Sports Illustrated*, and *The Rocket Magazine*, in her piece titled "Defending Tyson: The Bite Fight," she writes about the second Mike Tyson-Evander Holyfield fight.

The date was June 28, 1997, and the MGM Grand, Las Vegas, the place. Tyson and Holyfield were fighting for the World Boxing Association heavyweight championship.

According to Dunn, "The sanctified Holyfield was fighting dirty. He was hitting low and holding and hitting from the moment the bell rang for the first round."

Too, he was "butting repeatedly and intentionally."

In round two, a butt from Holyfield opened a cut under Tyson's right eye. In round three, after Holyfield was staggered by a Tyson left hook to the chin, he "slammed the right side of his head against the cut on Tyson's eye."

Tyson retaliated by biting Holyfield's right ear, and moments later stunned him with a right hook. Holyfield reacted by butting Tyson again. Then Holyfield's left ear felt Tyson's wrath.

What Tyson was doing, Dunn writes, was "following a long-standing boxing tradition: if you're fouled, foul in return."

Referee Mills Lane had seen enough and disqualified Tyson.

Dunn believes Lane did nothing to stop Holyfield's tactics because he was one of Holyfield's biggest fans. Several months before the fight, she writes, he called Tyson "a vicious criminal who should never be allowed to box."

Yes, Dunn says, "the bites were impulsive," and "Tyson shouldn't have done it, but obviously he couldn't rely on Mills Lane to prevent Holyfield from butting."

The next day, Tyson apologized and said that "he would accept without contest whatever punishment the commission handed out. He asked not to be suspended for life. He didn't blame Holyfield or Mills or anyone else. He took total responsibility for his action...."

In Tyson's autobiography, *Undisputed Truth* (2013), written with Larry Sloman, he writes that after continually being butted in his second fight with Holyfield, "I snapped," that "I was an undisciplined soldier," and that "[I want to ask] the people who expected more from Mike Tyson to forgive me for snapping in the ring and doing something I have never done before and will never do again."

Whoa! Guess what? Research paid off for Dunn and Tyson. They learned that as an amateur Holyfield had once bitten an opponent.

Tyson discovered that Holyfield, eighteen years old at the time, was fighting Jakey Winters and had been knocked down with a "left hook to the body and a left to the head."

When Holyfield was back on his feet, Tyson writes, "he clinched Winters, spit out his mouthpiece, and took a bite out of [Winters'] shoulder, drawing blood. Winters pulled back in pain and screamed. And then the bell rang. The referee took a point away from Holyfield."

The decision, which was unanimous, went to Winters. "The only consequence Holyfield faced from his bite was," Tyson writes, "a bruised ego and a unanimous decision against him."

One of the most noteworthy points in Tyson's book is when he compares his image as a fighter—most people at the time wrongly considered him a thug—with Holyfield's.

"Part of the problem," he wrote, "was that people were responding to images, not reality. If you watched a tape of the fight, you'd see that Holyfield was clearly fighting a dirty fight, but he had a good guy image. He was the one who strolled into the ring singing gospel songs."

WHAT STANDS OUT FOR ME (3)

In Anne Patchett's book of essays, *Those Precious Days*, is her Introduction, "Essays Don't Die." In it, she speaks for anyone who likes to write: "It's a wonderful thing to go back to something that's a couple of years old, see the flaws in the fullness of time, and then have the chance to make corrections and polish it up—or in some cases throw the whole thing out and write a better version."

She adds that she's "always writing essays," though she admits they "never filled my days, but they reminded me that I was still a writer when I wasn't writing a novel."

Later in the book, Patchett, co-owner of the Parnassus Bookstore in Nashville, Tennessee, says that she's "pretty much the poster child for how to incorporate the humanities into your life. It is my greatest love, my deepest joy, and all I want to do is share it, to use books and writers to bridge the lonely technological divides we find ourselves stuck in.

"I believe I've done more good on behalf of culture by opening Parnassus than by writing novels. I've made a place in my community where everyone is welcome.

"As every reader knows, the social contract between you and a book you love is not complete until you can hand that book to someone else and say, *Here, you're going to love this.*"

…about Truman Capote's *A Capote Reader* (1987) is Capote's theory about writing—specifically, when he makes the reader aware of how important it is to be selective and having the confidence in what you've been selective about.

As a child, Capote says, "I played a pictorial game. I would, for example, observe a landscape—trees and clouds and horses wandering in the grass—then select a detail from the overall vision, say grass bending in the breeze, and frame it with my hands."

The book's most notable passage is when Capote writes that "…this detail became the essence of the landscape and caught, in prismatic miniature, the true atmosphere of a panorama too sizable to encompass otherwise." That detail "seemed of itself to contain the secret. All art is composed of selected detail, either imaginary or, as *In Cold Blood*, a distillation of reality."

…about Audrey Hepburn's starring role in William Wyler's *Roman Holiday* (1953): It was her breakthrough movie and first lead, and she earned the year's Oscar for Best Actress.

The movie is about a British princess named Ann who decides to escape from her embassy to experience life in Rome. There, she meets streetwise reporter Joe Brady (Gregory Peck). After Brady learns she's a princess, he pretends to be ignorant of her true identity.

The reason? He's after an exclusive.

In the movie's most indelible scene, Hepburn isn't acting. Gary Fishgall in *Gregory Peck*, a biography of the actor, explains, "The reporter and the princess encounter a wall bearing an ancient, sculptured face with an open mouth. The reporter dares her to stick her hand in the opening, warning her that, according to legend, the creature will bite off the hand of anyone who is lying. Since neither he nor she has been completely honest with the other, the prospect is intimidating."

Before filming the scene, Peck "suggested to Wyler that he keep the gag going by pulling his arm out with his hand hidden in the sleeve of his suit jacket." Wyler loved the idea but told Peck not to tell Hepburn about it.

Peck: "Keeping her in the dark is what made the scene work.... Her startled look of surprise leaps off the screen. She screams then dissolves into laughter."

FIGHTING LIKE A CHALLENGER

For fifty years, [Dave Kindred] tended to the craftsman's precision. He captured what other writers didn't because he abided by a credo of his own making. If you pay attention, you'll see something you've never seen before.
    —John Schulian, quoted in *The Great American Sports Page*

From Jimmy Cannon to Dave Kindred, from John Schulian to forty-three other sports journalists, *The Great American Sports Page* (The Library of America) features essential columns on horse racing, boxing, baseball, gymnastics, football, and golf. Most of the dispatches were written under a deadline.

Schulian, the author of the terrific *Writers' Fighters*, is the *Sports Page*'s editor and also a contributor; Charles P. Pierce penned the foreword.

Of the columns devoted to the sweet science, my favorites are Schulian's reflections on Marvelous Marvin Hagler's war with Tommy Hearns, Cannon's take on Billy Graham's fight against Kid Gavilan, and Kindred's report on Willie Pastrano after he retired from boxing.

WAR

Consider Schulian's "The Proud Warrior." The scene is Las Vegas, Caesars Palace, the date April 15, 1985: it's Marvin Hagler versus Tommy Hearns for Hagler's middleweight title.

It was the kind of fight boxing fans never tire of reading and talking about or watching time and again on YouTube. Pure action!

Schulian makes three key points about the fight:

First, in the opening round, "suddenly [Hagler] was jerked out of 1985 and back to a time when warriors wore loincloths instead of boxing trunks and did their hunting without benefit of eight ounce gloves. He was primitive, and that splash down the middle of his face wasn't blood. It was war paint."

Hyperbole? No! If you saw the fight, you know Schulian is spot on.

Second, in the third and final round, Schulian writes, "Every time Hearns tried to step to safety, Hagler was there punching him—punching, punching, punching until the spidery challenger must have thought he was trapped in a thunderstorm of leather."

Third, there's Hagler's sage reaction after the fight: "Yeah, I'm still the champion. But I had to fight like a challenger."

BILLY AND THE KID

Cannon's column "You're Billy Graham" is a tribute to one of the great welterweight contenders of the 1950s and focuses on his disputed fifteen-round decision loss to the great Kid Gavilan at Madison Square Garden in 1951.

Gavilan was the world welterweight champion, while Graham, who possessed one of the best left jabs of his era, was the number one challenger.

When the decision was announced in favor of Gavilan, boxing writers and fight fans were in shock.

"All the ringside writers unanimously scored it in Billy's favor and called him the new champion of the world," Willie Pep writes in his outstanding *Friday Night Heroes*. "The thousands who witnessed this great bout all pointed to Graham as the winner and new champ….If ever there was a fight that the decision should have been reversed, this was it…"

In a career that began in 1941 and lasted until 1955, Graham compiled a 102-15-2 (twenty-seven KOs) record. He was never knocked down or out.

"You're Billy Graham who was a champion," Cannon concludes, "but it isn't in the book."

SADDEST

IN 1980, DAVE KINDRED PENNED A COLUMN ABOUT WILLIE Pastrano, a former light heavyweight champion in the 1960s, for the *Washington Post*.

Titled "Willie Pastrano," it's the most heartbreaking piece in *The Great American Sports Page*.

After challenger Jose Torres dethroned him on March 30, 1965, at Madison Square Garden—he wasn't allowed to come out for the ninth round—Pastrano, who was born in New Orleans and began fighting professionally in 1951, retired with a 62-13-8 (fourteen KOs/ two KO 'by) record.

"For three years," Kindred writes, "Pastrano used heroin daily." But, he told Kindred, "It wasn't the heroin I wanted. It was the boxing ring….Boxers have been to war and are psychologically scarred. You get fighters acting like they're punch drunk when they're not, just to get attention…With the applause, you come to life."

Like a drug, the adulation a boxer receives in the ring can become addictive and is one reason why many fighters who should retire don't.

In 1969, Kindred writes, Pastrano "went cold turkey." What followed were "years of wandering. Las Vegas, Oklahoma City, Miami. A trail of tears…and Willie Pastrano, once a champion of the world…worked as a bouncer in strip joints, two o'clock in the afternoon 'til two the next morning, six days a week. Worked some as a chip runner in Vegas, did some greeting at a greasy spoon in Reno."

Pastrano died on December 6, 1997, age sixty-three.

THEIR PROSE

Churchill and Orwell is the book's title. Published in 2017, its author is Pulitzer Prize winner Thomas E. Ricks, a journalist and author who writes mainly about military and national security matters.

The book's most appealing and relevant aspect, for me, is what Ricks wrote about the writing styles of these two giants.

A sample of Orwell's writing: "*Hamlet* is the tragedy of a man who does not know how to commit a murder. *Macbeth* is the tragedy of a man who does.…*Macbeth* is the only one of Shakespeare's plays in which the villain and the hero are the same character."

Concise. Informative. Insightful. No frills. Shakespeare would be proud!

Next, check out Orwell's rules about writing:

- Never use a long word where a short one will do.
- If it is possible to cut a word out, always cut it out.
- Never use the passive where you can use the active.
- Never use a foreign phrase, a scientific word, or a jargon word if you can think of an everyday English equivalent. His last rule is the best one:
- Break any of these rules sooner than say anything outright barbarous.

Turning to Winston Churchill, Ricks writes that he once "[coached members of his staff] on writing reports. He found time on August 19, 1940, during the Battle of Britain, to issue a direction on brevity: 'The aim should be reports which set out the main points in a series of short, crisp paragraphs.'"

In February 1944, he advised President Franklin D. Roosevelt that "'it is nearly always better to cut out adverbs, and adjectives, too.'"

More, Churchill has the admirable ability to "compress an image into a small phrase, as when he refers to 'the scaly wings' of defeat that flapped over Germany in the interwar period."

Interestingly, there are instances when, Rick writes, "his prose can have the reassuring tone of an adult reading aloud to a loved child."

Listen carefully: On rare occasions, Ricks writes, Churchill's prose style was ornate. For example, during the 1930s he once wrote that "the British were content with frothing pious platitudes while foemen forge[d] their arms." Whoops!

"Most of the time," Ricks assures us, Churchill's writing "is sure and solid," and here's proof: "When does one first begin to remember? When do the waving lights and shadows of dawning consciousness cast their print upon the mind of a child? My earliest memories are Ireland. I can recall scenes and events in Ireland quite well, and, sometimes dimly, even people."

That's the way he begins *My Early Life*, his autobiography.

Every time I mention Winston Churchill, Gary Oldman comes to mind.

IKE IS SEARCHING FOR IKE

Although he was unhinged and very unpredictable as a person, in the ring, [Ike Ibeabuchi] was about as collected as you could be. The only time he seemed to find normalcy was in a profession that is not normal at all.

—Eric Bottjer, boxing matchmaker

PUNCHES THROWN

ONE OF THE MOST TELLING PASSAGES IN LUKE G. WILLIAMS' powerful, hugely readable *President of Pandemonium: The Mad World of Ike Ibeabuchi* (Hamilcar Noir/2021) is when he writes that the talented, troubled Nigerian heavyweight's exposure "to repeated head trauma may have aggravated or even caused some of his episodes of apparent bipolar disorder. Before the [David] Tua fight, it should be noted, Ibeabuchi had displayed signs of erratic behavior, but it had not descended into criminality. The American psychiatrist Dr. Daniel Amen has argued that 'traumatic brain injury is a major cause of psychiatric illness that ruin people's lives. . . .'"

Williams continues, "Against Tua—believed by many to be one of the hardest punchers in his heavyweight era—Ibeabuchi absorbed an astonishing number of hard punches."

Tua "landed two hundred power punches," according to Bob Canobbio of Compubox. "That fight may have been the beginning of the end for Ibeabuchi mentally. It might have started him on the route to all the problems he had."

STATS

Born in 1973, Ibeabuchi, who made his professional boxing debut in 1994, fought the highly ranked, powerful punching Tua on June 7, 1997, in the Arco Arena in Sacramento, California. Tua was an overwhelming favorite, which was why only 3,378 people showed up to watch what many boxing journalists later called "an instant classic."

Both fighters were undefeated: Tua was 27-0 (twenty-three KOs) and Ibeabuchi 16-0 (twelve KOs). According to Compubox, and this stat is almost unbelievable, "Ibeabuchi versus Tua featured more punches thrown than any other previous [heavyweight] bout, a stunning 1,730 in twelve rounds....Ibeabuchi threw 975."

(In 1975's "Thrilla in Manilla [Ali versus Frazier], 1,591 punches were thrown in fourteen rounds"....In 2019, the Ibeabuchi vs Tua punch total was broken in the Adam Kowacki versus Chris Arreola fight, where 2,172 were thrown.)

MERCHANT AND LAMPLEY, IBEABUCHI AND TUA

HBO commentator Larry Merchant said the "Ibeabuchi versus Tua fight was one of the best heavyweight fights of modern times," and sportscaster Jim Lampley believed it "was right up there with the 1992 Holyfield-Bowe fight."

Williams, who resides in South London and is a regular contributor to the Boxing Social website, writes that after the fight Ibeabuchi said that "...Mr. Tua was a durable fighter, [but] no doubt in my mind, if I had reduced the number of punches thrown and had sat on them maybe I would have been able to knock him out."

Tua, always gracious, said, "The decision was fair....I got away from my game plan a couple of times and that was my downfall.... His jabs gave me trouble."

NO HELP

As for Ibeabuchi's lack of mental stability, Eric Bottjer believes that "because he was a world-class boxer and because he had the potential to generate a lot of money, nobody tried to help him or protect the people around him that he was capable of hurting."

At the same time, "any sympathy for Ibeabuchi was tempered by an impact statement," Williams writes, that one of the boxer's sexual assault victims wrote: "The man made a permanent impact on my life. One day, hopefully, I'll be able to get some help and be able to put the fear this man brought in my life to rest. But until then, sleepless nights, flashbacks...is all I have now."

Also, consider the following remarks Ibeabuchi made about himself: "I'm not suffering from any psychological or mental ailment," and "How can I have the audacity to rape someone I'm paying to have sex with? In Nigeria, I wouldn't be in prison for what I did. The system here [in the United States] makes sure someone gets punished whenever a woman cries."

FREE AGAIN. BUT THEN...

In Williams' interview with Ibeabuchi on February 17, 2016, he explains that "throughout the entire conversation, Ibeabuchi gave an endearingly mild-mannered and friendly impression, which is of course at odds with the image of a crazed and unhinged monster that the media has so often created."

When Williams asked Ibeabuchi "how it felt to be free again after being in custody so long," he replied that he won't be free until he steps back into the ring.

Fifty days after Williams' interview, Ibeabuchi "was back in prison."

Though Ibeabuchi's dream is to return to the ring and become heavyweight champion, Williams concludes that "for Ike Ibeabuchi, the dream will never come true....But it won't die either."

W. C. HEINZ AT HIS BEST

Heinz is not just one of the great sportswriters this country has produced, but he is one of the great American writers.

Mike Lupica, quoted in *New York Daily News*

In a time when New York newspaper readers were blessed with Red Smith, Jimmy Cannon, and Frank Graham as sports columnists, Bill Heinz was as good as, and often better than, any of them.

Dave Anderson, quoted in *New York Times*

SIMPLY THE BEST

W. C. Heinz's *The Top of His Game* (2015) is a big, informative book weighing in at 585 pages—a true heavyweight. The tome contains Heinz's best, most memorable sports writing. Bill Littlefield did the editing.

And, yes, a large number of Heinz's contributions are about professional boxers, including Sugar Ray Robinson and Norman Rubio.

There are many examples of Heinz's prose that endear me to his writing. For example, take his lead in the piece on Robinson titled

"The Greatest, Pound for Pound": "When I am old, I wrote more than twenty years ago, 'I shall tell them about Sugar Ray Robinson. When I was young, I used to hear the old men talk of Joe Gans and Terry McGovern and Kid McCoy. They told of the original Joe Walcott and Sam Langford, of Stanley Ketchel and Mickey Walker and Benny Leonard. How well any of them knew these men I'm not sure, but it seemed to me that some of the greatness of these fighters rubbed off on these others just because they lived at the same time.'"

TWO GREATS

Sugar Ray Robinson and Willie Pep are two fighters Heinz greatly admired: Pep, he writes, "was the greatest creative artist I ever saw in a ring, [and] Sugar Ray Robinson remains the greatest fighter, pound-for-pound and punch-for-punch...."

In one of the best comparisons I've read about the two fighters, Heinz says that "Pep was a poet, often implying, with his feints and his footwork, more than he said....Robinson was the master of polished prose, structuring his sentences, never wasting a word...."

RAY'S SISTERS TO THE RESCUE

Rocky Graziano must've fought on the New York City streets every day. Jake LaMotta too. But the young Walker Smith Jr., who later became Sugar Ray Robinson, had a different idea about street fighting. He told Heinz that as a youngster living in Detroit and later New York, "I would avoid fightin', even if I had to take the short end...."

More: "I got to be known as a coward, and my sisters used to fight for me. They used to remark that they hoped someday I'd be able to take care of myself."

Robinson's dislike of fighting carried over to his professional boxing career, which began in 1940 and ended twenty-five years later.

"You may find this hard to believe, but I've never loved fightin'," he told Heinz. "I really dislike it.....Fightin', to me, seemed barbaric."

Responding to Heinz's point that "fighting has given you the most satisfying experiences you have ever known," Robinson said, "That's right. I enjoy out-thinkin' another man and out-maneuvering him, but I still don't like to fight."

IMAGINE! 174 VICTORIES!

BORN MAY 3, 1921, ROBINSON DIED ON APRIL 12, 1969. WHEN he retired from professional boxing, his astonishing record was 174-19-6 (109 KOs/one KO 'by). He was the world welterweight champion from 1946 to 1951 and the middleweight king five times. In 1990, he was inducted into the International Boxing Hall of Fame.

HEINZ INTERVIEWS WELTERWEIGHT NORMAN RUBIO

MY ONLY CRITICISM OF LITTLEFIELD'S SELECTIONS IN *THE Top of His Game* is he didn't include Heinz's "The Opponent" chapter from *Once They Heard the Cheers* (1979), a terrific book of interviews with retired professional athletes.

In "The Opponent," Heinz interviewed welterweight Norman Rubio, who was born in Arecibo, Puerto Rico, and began fighting in 1940. When he retired in 1948, he had compiled a 54-23-8 (nine KOs /three KO 'by) record.

Heinz interviewed Rubio at the former fighter's home in High Ridge in Columbia County, New York, in the 1970s and asked if he wanted his sons to become boxers.

"No, I wouldn't want it," Rubio replied. "You're like a racehorse, on a continuous training schedule from the time you get up in the morning until you go to bed. You're on special food all the time. You ain't supposed to have a girlfriend. So, what kind of life is that? It's inhuman."

Heinz asked Rubio about his two fights against Sugar Ray Robinson. Their first bout was on March 20, 1942, at Madison Square Garden, and Rubio was stopped in the seventh round.

In their second fight four years later at Roosevelt Stadium in New Jersey, Robinson won a ten-round decision.

HEINZ: How about Robinson?

RUBIO: A good fighter.

HEINZ: The best I ever saw.

RUBIO: Yeah, but you know something? Everybody, the referee and judges and everybody, always looked at what he did, and they always leaned his way. You know?

HEINZ: You went ten rounds with him, but in the first fight, he knocked you out in the seventh?

RUBIO: They stopped the fight on a cut.

HEINZ: You were never counted out?

RUBIO: Never. Always cuts.

HEINZ: They don't show today.

RUBIO: I had the scar tissue removed.

HEINZ: When you fought Robinson, did you go in really thinking you could beat him?

RUBIO: You see, you're in the ring every day. It's like you eat food every day, and the guy you're fighting is just another person. You say, 'Tonight's pay night.' I didn't know if I could beat anybody until I was in the ring."

NAMES AND CASTING IN BULL DURHAM

MONIKERS

Before becoming a director and screenwriter, Ron Shelton was a minor league professional baseball player, and now he's written a book, the excellent *The Church of Baseball* (2022).

In his best known movie, 1988's *Bull Durham*, which is partially based on Shelton's minor league baseball experiences, he writes about browsing through a Carolina League record book and coming across "some guy [who] hit fifty doubles in 1948; that's a ton of doubles, a lot more than I hit—and the name of the player jumped off the page as well: Lawrence 'Crash' Davis. That was the best baseball player nickname I'd ever heard: 'Crash.' That became the name of a character I hadn't yet invented. I had one of my principal characters, even if it was just a name. Names matter. Crash Davis felt like someone I knew, someone I could write. He felt a little like me."

A few evenings later, while he was dining at the Radisson Hotel in North Carolina, his server, "a large-framed, open-faced, sweet young man fresh out of waiter training school," introduced himself: "Hi there. My name's Ebby Calvin LaRoosh, but you can call me Nuke."

Shelton asked how he spelled his nickname because, for him, "there was only one Newk, the great Dodgers pitcher Don Newcombe, but I wanted to check."

N-U-K-E was the waiter's answer.

"I had my pitcher," Shelton says.

Shelton says he "changed 'LaRoosh' to 'LaLoosh' to distinguish it from Lyndon LaRouche, the strange, cultlike leader of a Marxist movement of the time. I may not have had a story, but I had a battery—a pitcher and a catcher—and they even had good, solid baseball names."

The movie's third major character and its narrator was Annie Savoy. If you're wondering where her name came from, Shelton writes that "baseball groupies have traditionally been called 'Annies'—a name that sounds warm and unthreatening..."

After Shelter had typed in Annie, he spotted a matchbook cover on his desk with the name "SAVOY" on it. Shelton had Annie's last name.

CASTING

After Kevin Costner, whose film career was on the rise, was cast as Crash Davis, Tim Robbins, Shelton writes, "was available and everyone liked him, but I wouldn't make a commitment until I put him in a room with Kevin to see how they played off each other....Their different physicalities, manners, and voices suggested they could play together."

A meeting was arranged with Susan Sarandon, who had been living in a small town in Italy. When she arrived in New York, "she flashed into the room looking brilliant....She wore a tube dress with four-inch red and white horizontal stripes that announced her presence with authority. Brassy, funny, physical, and off book. She didn't need script pages in her hand. She knew the character. She *was* the character.…We had a cast."

HALL

BEFORE ROBBINS WAS CAST AS NUKE, ANTHONY MICHAEL Hall was considered for the role. Shelton thought it "was an inspired idea and possibly a perfect foil for Costner's world-weary Crash."

His meeting with Shelton took place in New York at the Columbus Bar and Restaurant on Broadway.

Accompanied by eight friends, Hall arrived late. After the usual small talk, he told Shelton that "I haven't read [the script] yet."

Fortunately for Hall, Shelton believed in second chances. He and Hall met again a few days later.

"This time he showed up with half his possessions, which was a hopeful improvement, at least," Shelton writes.

When Shelton asked him what he "thought of the script and the character of Ebby Calvin 'Nuke' LaLoosh," Hall said, "I'm only up to page forty. Maybe thirty-five. We can talk about that."

Shelton stood up, he writes, and "left the table without saying a word."

THE ELITE OF THE ELITES

My first recollections of Willie Pep date back to 1965/1966. My grandfather, who adored the fighter, put me to sleep with bedtime stories about the elite boxer. Years later, as fate may have it, I spent considerable time--including an entire day on July 7, 1995--with Pep. I promised the boxer that I would one day write a book about him. I kept that promise as a salute to the centennial of his birth.

—Mark Allen Baker, boxing historian

Born on September 19, 1922, in Middletown, Connecticut, Guglielmo Papaleo, better known as Willie Pep and nicknamed the "Will-o'-the-Wisp," fought professionally from 1940 to 1966, was twice world featherweight champion, and compiled an amazing record of 229-11-1 (sixty-five KOs).

He owns two untouchable winning streaks. As Mark Allen Baker points out in his tenth boxing book, the meticulously researched, superbly written *Willie Pep: A Biography of the 20th Century's Greatest Featherweight* (McFarland Books), "His mark of not one, but two, winning streaks, each over sixty victories, will never be matched or surpassed."

A superior wordsmith, Baker doesn't dwell on Pep's personal life, but does skillfully summarize it: "Once your reflexes and legs go, a fighter's friends soon follow; he was a champ who lived like one; he was insolvent thanks to fast women, slow horses, and generous judges; he had only himself to blame for his financial condition, never anyone associated with his career...."

In 1990, Pep was inducted into the International Boxing Hall of Fame, and in 2005, welcomed into the Connecticut Boxing Hall of Fame.

Also, he's an author. With Robert Sacchi, he penned the memorable *Friday's Heroes* (1973).

RAY ROBERTS

PEP'S FORTY-SECOND AMATEUR FIGHT TOOK PLACE IN NOR-wich, Connecticut, in 1938, at the Duwell Athletic Club. His opponent, a tall, rangy, handsome youngster called Ray Roberts, outweighed Pep by close to twenty pounds.

Pep lost the three-round decision.

"It took every ounce of energy for the Hartford fighter to make the distance," Baker writes.

Roberts later became Sugar Ray Robinson—he was born Walker Smith Jr.—and was perhaps the greatest pound-for-pound boxer in the history of the sport.

As an amateur, Pep put together a 59-3-3 record. In 1938, he won the Connecticut State Amateur Flyweight Championship, and in 1939, the Connecticut State Bantamweight Championship. He was, Baker writes, "in a class by himself."

ANGOTT AND SADDLER

PEP WAS TWENTY YEARS OLD WHEN HE WON THE FEATH-erweight title from Chalky Wright at Madison Square Garden on September 20, 1942, before nineteen thousand fans.

With the victory over Wright he became, Baker writes, "the youngest featherweight champion since Terry McGovern over four decades ago." Pep and Wright fought three more times, with Pep winning two by decision and one by KO.

He went on to win sixty-two straight fights before losing a unanimous ten-round decision to tough veteran Sammy Angott, the former lightweight champion, in 1943 at MSG.

Pep's title wasn't at stake against Angott.

Six years later Pep, who had won seventy-three consecutive fights after losing to Angott, was a 3-1 favorite when he lost his title to Sandy Saddler, who stopped him in the fourth round at MSG.

A year later, in their rematch, again at MSG, Pep outboxed Saddler to regain the title.

In 1950, on September 8 at Yankee Stadium, Saddler reclaimed the title by stopping Pep, who had dislocated his shoulder in the seventh round and couldn't come out for the eighth.

Then in 1951, on September 26 at the Polo Grounds, Saddler again stopped Pep, this time in the ninth round. Over thirty-eight thousand fans were in attendance.

In *Friday's Heroes*, Pep writes that the fourth fight was "a real brawl...with wrestling, heeling, eye gouging, tripping, thumbing—you name it....Now a lot of people think there was antagonism between Sandy and me. Maybe there was during our fights—but we're friendly now...When we were fighting for the championship, I wanted to lick him in the worst way, and he wanted to lick me. Well, we went all out."

"Prior to the stoppage," Baker writes, "[referee Ray] Miller had Pep ahead 5-4 on rounds, 10-6 on points; judge Arthur Aidala scored it 4-4-1 on rounds, and Pep ahead on points 8-6; and judge Frank Forbes saw Saddler ahead 5-4 on rounds and 7-5 on points.... The right eyelid of Pep was so badly torn in the second round that the blood flow could not be contained—it blinded him in every subsequent session.

"In retrospect, it was one of the dirtiest fights in the history of boxing," Baker notes. "Every trick in the book was used."

SKILLS AND PHOTOS

IN BAKER'S APPENDIX, "SKILLS OVERVIEW," HE ACCESSES Pep's many skills, including his balance, footwork, spin move, and left jab.

Baker calls Pep's left jab his "guidance system," though "it wasn't as exciting as his left hook....It was often the precursor to destruction. He used it to direct his opponents into position, create an opening, or launch a window, if you will, before firing his heavier artillery. Because it was quicker, used less energy, and could be executed while moving, it was the elite fighters' prolific punch."

Those photos! Magnificent! More than seventy of them, including Pep with Alexis Arguello, sports journalist and scholar Sam Cohen, Jose Torres, and Muhamad Ali.

And for fans of Rocky Graziano and Jake LaMotta, two of Pep's closest friends, check out page 132.

There's one of a smiling Jackie Wilson, the Pacific Coast's lightweight and welterweight champion on page 75, and, of course, there are several of the great featherweight champion—and Pep's number one rival—the elite Sandy Saddler. (See pages 97, 114, 123, and 183.)

Glance at a 1954 photo of Angelo Dundee on page 127. As Baker notes, "[Dundee] admitted to teaching his fighters (Ali, Basilio, Foreman, etc.) many of the defense tactics used by the featherweight legend."

My favorite is the photo of an older, pensive Willie Pep on page 195. It was the last time he attended the Canastota Hall of Fame weekend.

A NAME IS A NAME IS A NAME

766 GOALS, 1555 ASSISTS

One unforgettable hockey moniker belongs to hockey Hall of Famer Jaromir Jagr, who played in the National Hockey League from 1990-91 to 2017-18. Fifteen of those seasons were with the Pittsburgh Penguins, three with the Washington Capitals, and four with the New York Rangers.

His best offensive season was in 1995-96 when he tallied sixty-two goals and had eighty-seven assists for 149 points in eighty-two games for the Penguins.

He and the great Mario Lemieux were two reasons why the Penguins won two consecutive Stanley Cups, the first in 1990-91, the second in 1991-92. Another reason for the Penguins' success was the acquisition, in a 1990-91 trade with the Hartford Whalers, of center Ron Francis, the Whalers' best player.

It was the worst trade in the Whalers' history but one of the best the Penguins ever made.

Jagr, who wore number sixty-eight, retired from professional hockey with 766 goals and 1,555 assists for a total of 1,921 points in 1,733 games. Among his awards were three Art Ross trophies, awarded to the player who led the NHL in total points at the end of the season.

MAYBE IT'S A MISPRINT

HERE'S ANOTHER GREAT HOCKEY NAME: WACEY RABBIT.

Rabbit, who is of First Nations descent and born in Lethbridge, Alberta, played professional hockey from 2001 to 2020. Five of those years were spent in the American Hockey League and six in the Western Hockey League.

He also played in Europe for several seasons with a number of different teams.

The first time I saw him play was for the American Hockey League Providence Bruins against the Hartford Wolf Pack in Hartford in 2006.

I was comfortably seated in my usual seat—a friend and I were season Wolf Pack ticket holders—and I was looking at the Bruins lineup in my program, and there glaring at me was the name Wacey Rabbit....A misprint. It must be. But it wasn't.

Rabbit was one of those good, dependable hockey players who had a long, productive career. After retiring as a player, he became an assistant coach of the Saskatoon Blades of the Western Hockey League.

FIRST NAMES

GROWING UP IN NEW HAVEN, I FOLLOWED THE EASTERN Hockey League New Haven Blades for many years during the mid-fifties, and for a while I was positive if you're a hockey player your first name had to be Ron.

You see, the Blades were packed for several seasons with Rons: Ron Rohmer, Ron Kapitan, Ron Foster, and Ron Telford.

Ron Telford, who wore number three and was the best defensive defensemen I ever saw, played for the Blades from 1955 to 1960 and was a perennial EHL All-Star.

Though he wasn't physical, he was able to put an opponent off balance with a carefully placed forearm to the chest, anticipate plays, see the entire ice, and play consistently excellent hockey.

He was one of the EHL's most skillful hockey players.

NEVER THE LEAD

One of the most recognizable actors of the 1940s and 1950s, Elisha Cook's movie career began in 1937. His last film was released in 1987.

Two of Cook's best movies starred Humphrey Bogart: John Huston's *The Maltese Falcon* (1940) and Howard Hawks' *The Big Sleep* (1946).

In *The Maltese Falcon*, he plays a cowardly thug named Wilmer. The direct opposite of his Harry Jones character in *The Big Sleep*, Cook's Wilmer talks tough but is no match for Bogart's Sam Spade, who at one point easily disarms him with several quick moves.

Yes, Jones is a two-bit criminal but a far better person than the gun-carrying, tough-talking Wilmer. He possesses courage and a sense of honor that Bogart's private eye Philip Marlowe admires because, courtesy of the vicious gangster Lash Canino, Jones sacrifices his own life to save his girlfriend's.

Cook handled both roles with conviction and credibility.

Something else about Cook is that I bet no other actor died more often in so many different ways than Cook did in his movies: He was shot, stabbed, strangled, poisoned, thrown out of windows, run over by cars and trains and trucks, strangled, stabbed, and shot—which I already mentioned, didn't I?

But he just kept coming back in a slew of motion pictures.

Another never-the-lead character actor was Thelma Ritter (1902-1969). Her film career began in 1947 and lasted until 1968.

With that great street-smart New York accent, no actor was better at cracking wise.

During her career, she was nominated six times for a supporting actress Oscar. In 1951, she took home the statuette for Best Supporting Actress for her performance as Alma in *Pillow Talk*.

In 1953's *Pickup on South Street*, which starred Richard Widmark and Jean Peters and was directed by Samuel Fuller, Ritter gave one of her most memorable performances as stoolie Moe Williams.

I'll speculate here about what Ritter would say regarding her character in *Pickup*: "In the scene moments before Moe is shot by the vicious Joey (Richard Kiley), we learn she's afraid and tired of looking over her shoulder for someone she ratted out who might sneak up on her.

"Moe knows she's soon going to die, and it'll be a relief from the kind of life she lives. At the same time, she's frightened of dying. I tried to blend her relief and her fear.

"The last time she's seen alive is in her small, cramped apartment with classical music playing on her record player.

"It was Sam Fuller's idea to have the streetwise Moe be a lover of classical music. It made her character more complex and human. That's why Moe, of the many characters I've played on the big screen, is one of my favorites."

ALWAYS DIFFERENT

The actor's art,/Can die and live, to act a second part.
   —William Shakespeare (Who else?), *Hamlet*

SWORD

MANY OF THE LATE BRITISH ACTOR NICOL WILLIAMSON'S coworkers claimed he was a hellraiser—unreliable, disruptive, unpredictable, even violent.

Take the incident that took place at the Walter Kerr Theater in April 1991, during the first act of *I Hate Hamlet*. It involved Williamson and Evan Handler, his costar. The two actors, who hadn't been getting along during rehearsals, were involved in a dueling scene when Williamson smacked Handler on his back with the flat of his sword.

That was it for Handler. He walked off the stage and exited the theater. His understudy would complete his role.

(The next day Handler handed in his notice.)

At the same time, Williamson had a kind side. Rewind to the 1978 revival of John Osborne's *Inadmissible Evidence*. Julia Peasgood was cast as the daughter of Williamson's Bill Maitland.

Gabriel Hershman, in *Black Sheep: The Authorised Biography of Nicol Williamson*, quotes her as saying that "Nicol was a consummate professional—dynamite on stage and kind and caring off. No one gave me more support than anyone I ever shared a stage with….I knew that whatever happened on stage with him I always felt safe."

CAINE AND CONNERY

IN HERSHMAN'S BIOGRAPHY, HE COMPARES THE ACTOR WITH audience favorites Michael Caine and Sean Connery and writes that "with Caine and Connery, you know what to expect. With Nicol Williamson, by contrast, you never knew what was coming."

I'll cite two movies illustrating Williamson's ability to inhabit characters fully different from each other. There's *Robin and Marian*, which stars Connery as Robin, Audrey Hepburn as Marian, Robert Shaw as the Sheriff of Nottingham, and Williamson as Little John.

The 1976 movie involves Robin and Little John's return from the Crusades to Sherwood Forrest after a twenty-year absence. Both men are middle-aged, tired, and battle weary.

Robin, who expects to take up where he left off with Marian, the love of his life, is in for a surprise because she's now an abbess of a Benedictine Nunnery in Kirklees, Yorkshire, and known as Mother Jennet.

The movie's most poignant scene occurs on the night Little John learns from Marian that Robin and his longtime enemy, the Sheriff of Nottingham, will engage in a duel the next morning.

When Marian entreats Little John to tell Robin not to fight the Sheriff, he says, "Say no to Rob? We've always been together. I'm nothing without him."

The scene's key moment occurs when we learn how Little John

feels about Marian. "You're Rob's lady," he says. "If you were mine, I never would've left."

The next morning, Robin slays the Sheriff.

As Little John helps his friend to his feet, the bloodied and seriously wounded Robin playfully asks him, "You're a stout fellow. What are you called?"

"They call me Little John," is his friend's response.

Perfect.

There's Williamson's turn as a manic Sherlock Holmes in *The Seven-Per-Cent Solution* (1976), which Herbert Ross directed. Williamson said that "my Holmes is different. The man is in the grip of a terrible affliction. The man is in a state of collapse."

Williamson's Holmes is, indeed, different from any of the actors who have previously portrayed the master detective on the big screen. He's frightening. He's often out control.

But at the end of the movie, thanks to Sigmund Freud (Alan Arkin), Holmes is on the road to recovery.

ESTEEMED CRITIC

FILM CRITIC PAULINE KAEL BLASTED WILLIAMSON, CALLING his performances "flamboyant…crude…violently self-conscious…. You feel as if he were trying to come out of the screen and strong arm you.…By his fifth movie, it's just about impossible to take his snarling and whinnying seriously…."

A tad harsh, Pauline.

And if she had in mind Williamson's fierce performance as Merlin in *Excalibur*, she might've overlooked, or perhaps didn't know, he enjoyed playing the master magician.

In *Black Sheep: The Authorised Biography of Nicol Williamson*, Gabriel Hershman quotes the actor as saying that "I tried to make him a cross between my old English master [Tom Reader] and a space traveler, with a bit of Grand Guignol thrown in."

Kael did praise Williamson's low-key supporting turn as the wealthy anthropologist William McCrory in Bob Rafelson's *Black Widow* (1987) as "enlivening" the movie.

REWIND

BACK TO THE WILLIAMSON-HANDLER INCIDENT. AFTER Handler's departure, Williamson, alone on stage, turned to the audience, and said, "Well, should I sing?" adding that "We'll begin the second act as quickly as possible."

NONE OF THAT GLAMOUR STUFF

In a recent article in the *New York Times* Theater section (Sunday June 18, 2023), Roslyn Sulcas writes that the great British actor Juliet Stevenson once said that if she "aspired to a Hollywood career," it would conflict with her personal life, that "I am not at ease in the industry and no good at all that glamour stuff. I never wanted to leave my children for long stretches while filming or acting outside the UK. But now my youngster is twenty-two, and I am free!"

Stevenson is best known, Sulcas writes, "for the 1990 Anthony Minghella film *Truly Madly Deeply*." The movie is, Sulcas believes, a "romantic comedy" about Stevenson's character, Nina, "mourning her dead lover."

Romantic comedy? I'm not sure about that. Set in England, the movie has comedic moments, but there's always the existence of Nina's immense grief over the death of her beloved Jamie, a cellist, played by the great Alan Rickman.

Nina, an interpreter, eventually comes to terms with Jamie's death, but not before he returns as a ghost, along with several of his ghost buddies.

Only Nina sees Rickman's character and his pals, which means it's safe to say he and they exist only in her mind.

A crucial scene takes place near the end of the movie when Nina is present at the birth of her friend's baby girl. Holding the newborn in her arms, she kisses her forehead, then looks into her eyes and says, "A new life."

There's a pause and, for the second time, she says, "A new life."

The first time Nina says "a new life" is for the newborn.

The second time is for herself: It's her realization that she must let go of Jamie and he of her, and that a new life beckons for her in the person of the effervescent Mark (Michael Mahoney), a psychologist and amateur magician.

The final scene in the movie is a coda: Jamie and his ghost pals are looking out the window of Nina's apartment, and they're smiling and waving at Nina and Mark.

One of Jamie's ghost friends says to him, "Well?" and Jamie responds, with a hint of sadness, "I think so."

WHAT STANDS OUT FOR ME (4)

s what I read in different newspapers concerning Bruce Cassidy and Jim Montgomery. Cassidy was the head coach of the National Hockey League Boston Bruins for six seasons, compiling an impressive 246-108-46 record. That didn't stop the Bruins from firing him before the 2022-2023 season began or the Las Vegas Golden Knights from hiring him for that season.

Hired to replace Cassidy was Montgomery, who guided the Bruins during the 2022-23 season to sixty-five wins, the most ever in NHL history.

Bruins' fans and pundits alike were positive the Boston team would win the Stanley Cup, professional hockey's biggest prize. To their dismay, Boston was eliminated in the first round by the underdog Florida Panthers.

What happened? A friend told me that "it was age! The Bruins aged right before our eyes." Pause. "Just jokin.'" Others hockey followers hold the hockey gods responsible because those rascals, believe in them or not, have a way of making weird things happen, especially in the playoffs.

The Panthers made it to the Stanley Cup finals where they played the Las Vegas Golden Knights, coached by, if you recall, Bruce Cassidy. In only their sixth NHL season, the Golden

Knights knocked off the Panthers in five games to win the 2022-2023 Stanley Cup.

…about Mel Brooks in *All About Me* (2021), his memoir, is how he handled his crew's reactions to many of the humorous scenes in 1974's *Young Frankenstein*.

He writes, "I was constantly reshooting because of the laughing from the crew. So, one day, I went out and bought a hundred white handkerchiefs."

Okay, Mel! Then what?

"I handed them out and said to the crew, 'If you feel like laughing, don't! Stick this handkerchief in your mouth.'"

Mel's plan worked: the next day, "I turned around once in the middle of reshooting a scene and saw a sea of white handkerchiefs in everybody's mouths."

…is Sherlock Holmes and Doctor Watson's meeting with Dr. Sigmund Freud in Nicholas Meyer's *The Seven-Per-Cent Solution* (1974).

At the doctor's Vienna home, Holmes introduces Dr. Freud to his powers of observation when he says, "You are married, possess a sense of humor, and enjoy playing cards and reading Shakespeare and a Russian author whose name I am unable to pronounce."

And he's not finished: "That you are a physician is clear to me when I glance at your medical degree on the far wall. That you no longer practice medicine is evident by your presence here at home in the middle of the day, with no apparent anxiety on your part about a schedule to keep."

Here's the part I liked best: "Your separation from various societies is indicated by those spaces on the wall, clearly meant to display additional certificates. The color of the paint there is somewhat paler in small rectangles, and an outline of dust shows me where they used to be."

(Holmes is never shy about displaying his observational talents, is he?)

But Freud, the novel's most admirable character, isn't intimated by Holmes and shouts that "this is wonderful!"

Eventually, Freud is able to help Holmes come to terms with his numerous problems, the most serious being what happened to the detective's parents when he and his brother Mycroft were children.

And yes, Dostoyevsky, who Jack Kerouac once said was "one of us," was the Russian writer whose name Holmes couldn't pronounce.

…is what Mark Allen Baker, in *Willie Pep: A Biography of the 20th Century's Greatest Featherweight*, writes about Pep's title defense against Eddie Compo.

When I was growing up in the Elm City, a popular boxing city in the 1940s and 1950s, Pep, Julie Kogon, Nathan Mann, and Compo were the fighters most often written about in the local papers, the *New Haven Register* and the *New Haven Journal Courier*, and talked about by boxing fans.

Unsurprisingly, weeks before the title bout at Waterbury's Municipal Stadium in 1949, the state's boxing fans were abuzz with excitement; after all, two Connecticut fighters, one a world champion, would be battling for the champion's title!

Born in Fair Haven, Connecticut, twenty-one years old, and one of the best featherweights in the division, Compo had an impressive 57-1-3 record.

Slightly more than ten thousand people were in attendance to watch Pep floor Compo twice in the fifth round and once in the seventh. After the third knockdown referee Billy Conroy wisely stopped the fight, though Compo was on his feet.

As Baker writes, "Compo was lucky to last as long as he did as the champion battered him unmercifully….Pep controlled the battle with his left jab and used his right cross to confirm his dominance."

Rick Biondi and Salvatore A. Zarra point out in their superb book, *Elm City Italians*, that "Despite the loss to Pep, Eddie was far from a spent fighter. Until he retired in 1955, he was a difficult opponent….On September 21, 1951, Compo bested an undefeated Chico Vejar at Madison Square Garden….The victory rejuvenated his career."

Compo retired in 1955 with a 75-10-4 record and was inducted into the Connecticut Boxing Hall of Fame in 2019. He passed away in 1999.

RAID-WORTHY

Consider carefully what you'll be reading because, yes, it involves:

- RAID
- Insect repellent
- Kills Flies and Mosquitoes
- Indoor and Outdoor
- No Lingering odors
- Net Wt. 15 oz.
- Outdoor Fresh Scent.

And mention has to be made that Raid must be kept away from children, thank you very much.

A few weeks ago, I was in dire need of Raid insect repellent. Amazon.com to the rescue. Price: $15.79. One click. My order was placed.

A few days later on a hot afternoon, I noticed sitting on our porch a large package beckoning to be opened.

(Maybe someone sent me some books.)

In manly fashion, I lugged the package upstairs, placed it on the dining room table, opened it, and inside was, yes, *one, two, three, four, five, yada, yada…twelve* cans of Raid.

Whoa! I had ordered one can. Pray tell, something is amiss. I dashed to my computer downstairs, hooked onto Amazon.com, went to the orders section, and there was my order—for one can of RAID at, as previously noted, $15.79.

I began mulling: Should I be honest and get in touch with Amazon and send the package back to the company?

Then the lie-to-yourself god kicked in (some folks might call it conscience) and said, "If you were to send back the package, whoever packed it would probably be fired, or at the least robustly reprimanded."

On the other hand, I thought, *maybe the packers for some ungodly reason picked me as the recipient of their day's act of kindness.*

Pause.

What do to? Then once again the lie-to-yourself god had something to say, and this time rather crankily: "Just find several friends who are Raid-worthy and give them one can from your precious collection. Keep three or four for yourself. Okay?"

I gave the gift of Raid to five friends who were surprised beyond words because they had never received insect repellent for a present.

Have you?

One friend, who loves to crack wise and can be a pain in the ass, smirkingly asked me, "Should I use this Raid stuff as an underarm deodorant, or, er, for insects?" and he laughed.

My faster than a speeding bullet response was: "Both, you arsehole!"

WHAT STANDS OUT FOR ME (5)

In British writer T. H. White's *The Book of Merlyn: The True Last Chapter of The Sword in the Stone* (1977), is, the discussion early on between Merlyn the Magician and King Arthur—they're both creaky old men—about adults and children and animals and readers.

King Arthur is momentarily puzzled.

"Readers?" he asks.

MERLYN: The readers of the book.
KING ARTHUR: What book?
MERLYN: The book we are in.
KING ARTHUR: Are we in a book?

Yes, Arthur, you and Merlyn, your trusted friend and mentor, make appearances in *The Book of Merlyn*.

Also, what stands out for me is Merlyn's skullcap, which was written about earlier in this book in the essay *Williamson's Magic Skullcap*. In the Berkeley Publishing Group edition of *The Book of Merlyn*, on page thirteen, White writes that Merlyn "[snatches] off his skullcap and [presents] it under Arthur's nose...."

Which proves Bob Ringwood, the costume designer of John

Boorman's *Excalibur*, read *The Book of Merlyn* and determined that a skullcap would enable Williamson to understand Merlyn better, so he created one for the actor.

Simple enough! Kudos to Mr. Bob Ringwood.

…about Claire Dederer's *Monsters*: *A Fan's Dilemma* are three of the thirteen well-known artists—mostly writers—about whom she writes.

Ernest Hemingway, Dederer says, "was a hitter, a beater-upper, an insulter. He decked friends and enemies alike." His fourth wife, Mary Hemingway, said "proudly at one point that 'it is more than a year since he hit me.'"

Doris Lessing "left two children behind when she moved from Rhodesia to London with the third," and that—and this is Dederer's most important point—"if the male crime is rape…the hardest-hearted woman isn't a murderer or rapist—she's a leaver of children."

Dederer first read *Lolita,* Nabokov's most famous book, when she was about thirteen, the same age as Lolita. She was horrified. How could anyone write a book about a child rapist? "Child rape," she writes, and correctly, "is not just a sexual act, but the thievery of childhood itself. The annihilation of personhood is the act's terrible trace."

Lolita's author, she believed, had to be a monster to create someone like Humbert Humbert!

As an adult, she re-read *Lolita,* researched Nabokov, and found that "there is no evidence at all that Nabokov himself was a pedophile in his inmost heart." What he did in *Lolita,* "in writing these dark desires, [was] reject the formula that genius deserves license. Greatness does not mean a free pass to do whatever you want."

What he did was "to write *as the monster.*"

I read Dederer's book because it's always a treat reading an author I haven't read before. Simultaneously, it's always a shock of sorts learning about immensely talented, famous individuals who are, with one exception, shits in their private lives.

And it was a relief to read the chapter about Nabokov.

…is what W. C. Heinz says in *Once They Heard the Cheers.* In the chapter titled "The Uncrowned Champ," he paid tribute to those journeymen fighters, and there are many of them, who "we so seldom celebrate" but "who are just honest workers, and yet it is they, and not the champions, who best represent and reflect us."

It's the most significant sentence in Heinz's book.

LONG OVERDUE

Despite [Althea Gibson's] status as the greatest female tennis player in the world [and] her crashing the white world of tennis, nothing really had changed at all. She remained as poor as she had been when she began.

—Sally H. Jacobs, *Althea: The Life of Tennis Champion Althea Gibson*

IT'S ABOUT TIME

YES, FINALLY A BIOGRAPHY OF ALTHEA GIBSON, THAT BRAVE and sometimes troubled phenomenal athlete. Raised on the tough streets of Harlem, she went on to be named the world's top-ranked female tennis player in 1957 and 1958.

Let's hope Sally H. Jacobs' smartly crafted, thoroughly researched *Althea: The Life of Tennis Champion Althea Gibson* brings Gibson the long overdue recognition she deserves.

The key passage in Jacobs' book is when she quotes Gibson, who in *I Always Wanted to Be Somebody*, her autobiography, wrote that "some sections of the Negro press resent my refusal to turn my tennis achievements into a rousing crusade for racial equality, brass band, seventy-six trombones, and all. I won't do it....I want my success to speak for itself as an advertisement for my race."

Gibson considered herself "a tennis player, not a Negro tennis player. I never set myself up as a champion of the Negro race.... Someone once wrote that the difference between me and Jackie Robinson is that he thrived as a Negro battling for equality whereas I shy away from it."

NOT A RAISED FIST...AND HEARTBREAK

JACOBS BELIEVES THAT GIBSON, WHO REGULARLY FACED racial discrimination during her tennis career, was correct to "let her success...speak for her and the potential of her race, rather than her raised fist."

But perhaps Gibson should've compromised and balanced the successes of her tennis career with well-timed remarks about the country's racial discrimination practices.

(Think of the metaphor about the greasy wheel.)

Turning to Jacobs' heartbreaking last chapter, "Not the Gibson Grandstand," Jacobs cites Darrell Fry's 1998 column for the *Tampa Bay Times*. In it, he sums up Gibson, long retired from tennis, in her sixties, impoverished, reclusive, and in poor health, as "in essence suffering from a broken spirit brought on by a long bout with life."

An almost forgotten trailblazer who shattered the color barrier in tennis, Althea Gibson paved the way for such greats as Arthur Ashe, Zina Garrison, and Serena and Venus Williams.

ABOUT THE AUTHOR

Born in New Haven, Connecticut, Roger Zotti somehow graduated from Hillhouse High School. With the passing of time, he was able to get his head on straight and graduate from Eastern Connecticut State College in 1966.

A master's degree from Wesleyan University in 1971 followed.

After teaching adult education at several Connecticut prisons for over twenty years, he retired in 1993. A regular contributor to the *International Boxing Organization Research Journal,* he also serves on its editorial board.

Hockey, reading, treadmilling, boxing, the WNBA *Connecticut Sun,* movies, music (old and new), watching British procedurals, and, of course, writing are among his interests.

He, his wife, and their creative dog live in Preston, Connecticut, and have two adult children, Tom and Leslie, and one grandson, Jake.

Contact him at rogerzotti@aol.com to say nice things about his writing.